ABOUT THE AUTHOR

"THERE ARE VERY FEW BORN STORYTELLERS.
K.M. PEYTON IS ONE OF THEM."
THE TIMES

KATHLEEN PEYTON started writing at the age of nine
and had her first book accepted for publication
when she was fifteen. While she was at school
in London, she daydreamed of owning her own
pony, and so horses became the subject of many of
her books.

Kathleen originally studied to become an artist,
but she also continued to write and has since had
more than fifty books published. She has won both
the Carnegie Medal and the Guardian Children's
Fiction Prize, and her best known books, the
original *Flambards* trilogy, were made into a
television series.

She now lives with her husband and her horses
near Maldon in Essex.

K.M.PEYTON

MINNA'S QUEST

USBORNE

To Linda

First published in the UK in 2007 by Usborne Publishing Ltd., Usborne House,
83-85 Saffron Hill, London EC1N 8RT, England. www.usborne.com

Copyright © K. M. Peyton, 2007

The right of K. M. Peyton to be identified as the author of this
work has been asserted by her in accordance with the
Copyright, Designs and Patents Act, 1988.

Cover photography: model supplied by Looks London Ltd./
photo by Steve Shott, background: Digital Vision.

Map by Ian McNee.

The name Usborne and the devices ♀ ⊕ are Trade Marks of
Usborne Publishing Ltd.

All rights reserved. No part of this publication may be reproduced,
stored in a retrieval system or transmitted in any form or by any means,
electronic, mechanical, photocopying, recording or otherwise without
the prior permission of the publisher.

This is a work of fiction. The characters, incidents, and dialogues
are products of the author's imagination and are not to be construed
as real. Any resemblance to actual events or persons,
living or dead, is entirely coincidental.

A CIP catalogue record for this book is available from the British Library.

JFMAMJJA OND/07 ISBN 9780746078815   Printed in Great Britain.

I

The foal lay out on the saltings where it had been thrown by a Roman soldier. It was very weak, near dead, which is why it had been abandoned. The distraught dam had been ridden out that morning on a raiding party and was now far away. The foal was alone. The crows circled overhead, waiting to peck out its eyes, and the tide was creeping up. The foal struggled to get up, but was too weak. The ground beneath him was cold and wet. Instinct told him that he lacked the vital needs to live, and he fought against it. His heart was large but his body weak.

After the useless struggle he lay still and closed his eyes.

A crow landed on his ribs and cawed with anticipation.

Minna looked down from the wooden quay which lay on the seaward side of the fort where she lived and saw the crow sitting on something that feebly moved. Minna had eyes like a hawk (she was used to being called by one of the lookouts to check a movement out at sea, although she was only a girl). She could make out the movement of the crow and knew its intention. She picked up a stone and threw it, hard and accurate, and the crow flew off with a squawk. The foal jerked as the stone hit it.

"Why, it's a foal!" She had thought it was a strayed sheep, fallen on its back like the stupid things often did. But a foal!... She jumped down from the quay and ran along the path under the wall, shouting for her brother Cerdic. He was collecting driftwood on the high-tide line and looked up at her shout.

"Come quick! Look!"

The alarm in her voice moved him and he followed her curiously across the saltings. They reached the foal together and could see immediately that it was dying.

"Poor thing! Whoever threw it here? The pigs!" Minna was outraged. She dropped to her knees and cradled the small head in her arms. The eyes opened, soft with exhaustion.

"We must carry it home, poor little thing!"

"It's rubbish – that's why it's been thrown out," said Cerdic. "Leave it."

"No!"

"They won't have it in the fort, you idiot."

"We'll take it to our hut in the vicus. Our mother won't throw it out."

"It's got no dam. How can it live?"

"I'll feed it milk and honey. I will make it live! And then it will be ours! Don't you see, they can't possibly ask for it back if we save it. We'll have a pony of our own."

Cerdic was swayed by this argument, she could see. He had always wanted a pony, to be like the soldiers in the fort. They were a cavalry legion and he could scarcely wait for the day when he would be old enough to enlist and ride with them. His best friend was the young Roman auxiliary, Theodosius, at seventeen three years older than himself.

"It's going to die, you can see. But it won't hurt to try, I suppose."

"We must take it now – the tide's nearly here. Can you lift it?"

Cerdic was strong but a foal, however sickly, was no light weight. It was some way to the vicus – the straggle of domestic huts and shops that lined the road that led inland away from the fort. One of them belonged to the children's family but they did not use it much, living in quarters inside the fort where their parents worked. It was used mostly for storage and animal feed and to house the plough and oxen harness – and the oxen too in the winter.

Cerdic kneeled down and between them they managed to lift the foal onto his shoulders. It made no struggle and lay so still that Minna was afraid it was already dead. She helped Cerdic stagger to his feet.

"It needs shelter. The wind is freezing."

She pulled her shawl round her shoulders, anxious now. Her mother would help her, she guessed, but her father...best he did not know. He had no reason to come to the vicus, busy at his work in the blacksmith's shop inside the fort. He was not given much to kindness.

"If this foal lives," Cerdic said through gritted teeth, "it will be mine. Remember that."

"Yes, yes. I don't mind. I shall make it live."

Minna did not heed the words, only too pleased to have got her brother to help. They came round the corner of the fort and onto the road from the gateway. This was the only way across the deep moat in front of the fort. The road here, as it led away inland, was lined with shops and houses, drinking dens and workshops, but Cerdic led the way through them to one of the huts that lay behind, built in the old style, half sunk in the ground, back to the wind, thatched heavily in reeds. This was their long-time family base, from the days when their great, great and more great grandparents eked a living selling farm produce to the garrison. Sometimes Minna wished they still lived here in the peace and quiet. But now their family was a part of the fort as much as the soldiers themselves and had living space allotted inside. Minna's parents had earned the authority's regard by their allegiance and the good work they turned out and they had proved they were a cut above the rabble that lived outside. But the hut was retained; it was warm out of the wind and there was a bed of thick straw where the oxen had been – not too dirty. Minna ran to a timber chest and pulled out some old blankets. Cerdic lowered the foal onto the straw and Minna wrapped it in the blankets.

"Ma'll kill you," Cerdic said.

"No. She'll help me. Will you tell her, if you're going back?"

Cerdic nodded and departed, scornful of women's things. Minna got down and lay against the foal to give it warmth. It was breathing. She could see its thin flanks fluttering, its little nostrils widening with the shallow breaths. She wrapped her arms round it, shedding tears as her cheek lay against the soft, cold fur. They had no heart, those soldiers. Theo was as bad as the rest, always beating his little mare to keep up. None of the cavalry horses were more than ponies, most only just big enough to keep their riders' feet off the ground. They called them horses, all the same. The men were proud of being cavalry rather than infantry, and slept with their horses inside the fort.

"Maybe your mother died?" Minna whispered. To bring up a foal without a dam was much too time-consuming for a serving soldier. But it was such a weakly thing, she could see. It would be hard to save.

"What's all this? Cerdic came with some tale about a foal…oh, gracious me! What have you got?"

It was her mother, thank goodness!

"They threw it out! It was lying on the saltings."

"Poor little duck. It's a pretty thing, but it will die for sure."

"Oh no! I will look after it, I promise. *Please...*"

"Oh, you silly child –"

But Minna knew her mother. For all her brisk manner she was soft inside like a honey cake. She would rescue birds from snares and butterflies from webs. Young homesick soldiers in the fort knew her kindness, for she understood how it was for an innocent young man to be thrown into the rough and tumble of barrack life, where cynical and embittered old soldiers enjoyed a newcomer to bait. She wasn't above scourging the older men with her tongue and taking the newcomer home for a quiet rest by their fireside. She was everyone's nurse at times of sickness and an inspired binder of wounds.

"It needs its mother's milk," Minna said.

"Yes, of course. But look at it – so puny! No wonder they threw it out. The dam has either died, or gone out on patrol as usual. I heard a deal of whinnying this morning when the patrol left, so I guess that's what happened. They took the foal away and forced the poor mare on her way. They have no heart, some of these boys! We'll do our best, Minna."

This meant fetching milk from the neighbour, warming it over the brazier in the metalwork shop, diluting it with water from the well, stirring thin honey from their own store into the jug and then, with infinite care, dripping it into the little mouth. Minna held the foal's head up and its mouth open, and her mother dribbled the food in very slowly. It seemed to take ages, and Minna, with a slightly sinking heart, knew that it was going to have to be repeated many, many times if the foal was to live. Even then…

"It's not the same as its own dam's milk. Don't bank on its living, Minna."

All the same, her mother did not chide Minna when she said she would stay by its side.

"It needs my warmth."

"You're a silly girl, but –" She laughed. "I can manage without you today. I'll tell your father I sent you on an errand."

"Cerdic's not working!"

Her mother laughed. "That's the way of the world, my dear."

"I'll sleep out here tonight."

"Yes, but don't be too upset when it dies."

She would ask Theo to help her when he came back, Minna decided. He could get her mare's milk from somewhere. He only had to command. He was like that, proud and bossy, cut out to be a commander – anyone could see that. Although he was so young, he was already in charge of eighty men. He was a stopgap, true, until someone older was appointed. The commander of the fort had been his father, but his father had died suddenly of an infection, and Theo had taken his place. It had seemed quite natural, as he had always been his father's shadow. And the men accepted him. They were a rough lot – auxiliaries from Africa and beyond, mostly black, some from Gaul, some from Rome, some from who knows where? – but he commanded and they obeyed. He too was from North Africa. He had another tongue besides the usual Roman and Celt. He had the nose of an Arab, the silky brown skin of an Egyptian, the black laughing eyes of a Roman girl and the poise of a Greek god. Minna adored him. She went giddy when he was near. Cerdic mocked her: "She's in love!" Minna was going to marry Theo one day, if only he knew! She would die otherwise. Unfortunately he wasn't interested in girls, only in being a soldier. Just like Cerdic.

The little foal slept. He wasn't dead, Minna could tell by the faint flutter in his nostrils. She tucked the blankets round him and lay all along his back, her head resting on his flank. She could feel the feeble rise and fall of his ribcage against her cheek. He might breathe away into death, she thought. Soon she must rouse him to another drink. She kept the pottery jug of milk and honey against her stomach under the blankets to keep it warm, but so soothing and quiet it was that she fell asleep.

She was woken by a convulsive shake of the foal beside her. It squeaked and threshed its poor legs in a hopeless effort to get up, thrusting Minna away. She started up, astonished, and was immediately aware of a shouting and commotion outside. A wild whinny rent the air. Minna thrust the blankets aside, knocking over the milk jug as she did so, so that she swore, but then ran without trying to rescue the precious food.

Outside she saw a cluster of people laughing round a loose pony. It was saddled and bridled but its gear was all awry, broken reins trailing, and it was almost white with lather. As someone caught it up and jerked at its bit to stop it, it flailed out with its back legs and sent people flying. It whinnied again, and Minna knew exactly what was happening: this was the foal's dam. She saw with one glance that it was a mare, and that milk was running from her in a stream down her back legs.

Minna ran to her head and caught the bridle. She shouted the stupid boys away, but turned to one, Stuf, she knew and said, "Help me! She must come to my hut, she's after her foal and it's in there. I've got it."

"She's from the patrol, she's dumped her rider," Stuf said. "Good on her!"

He helped Minna lead the mare to the shelter. Perhaps she smelled her foal, for she came willingly, trembling. Minna was terrified the foal might have died in its throes to get up, it was so weak, but when the mare came in through the door she saw that, although it was still down, its head was lifted. The funny little squeak came from its throat, to be returned by the mare with a frantic deep whickering, over and over. She pushed her captors aside and stood nuzzling at the foal, licking it and pushing at it quite roughly with her nose.

"It can't get up. We must help it," Minna said.

She couldn't believe this was happening: like a gift

from the gods! Wham, the return of riches, of succour, of life! Thank you, thank you, Zeus, Mithras, Jesus and all! She got her arms round the foal's chest and Stuf lifted it bodily from behind – he was a strong lad, built like an ox – and between them they pushed it to the mare's udder. It couldn't stand without their help and its suckling was almost too weak to take the milk, but the little mare, as if she understood, stayed quiet as an old sheep, only turning her head to gently lick the little foal's skinny flank.

"Don't let go," Minna said.

Was the foal too weak to suck? It was touch and go as to whether Minna must milk the mare herself and trickle the milk into the foal. But even as they stood there awkwardly they could gradually feel confidence seeping into the fragile newborn. Its sucking grew stronger: it had found at last what it had been yearning for!

"I'm sure it's going to live. It has such a will," Minna said.

"But it's such a puny thing! Of course they threw it out."

"Its body will grow. But it's got a big heart already, you can see. That's what matters."

"They won't let you keep the mare. Whose is it anyway? Someone's got a long walk home."

Minna did not want to think about this, because she was pretty sure the mare was none other than Pesrut, the mount of Theodosius, no less.

"I think it's the centurion's."

Stuf snorted with laughter. "Poor Theo! But of course, he won't walk. He'll take someone else's mount. But did he not know she'd foaled?"

Minna had told him days ago that she thought Pesrut was in foal but Theo had scoffed and said it was impossible. She hadn't been near a stallion. She had got fat and lazy because he fed her too well. He had to beat her to keep her in her rightful place at the head of his soldiers. He had told Minna he was going to order a better animal.

Minna knew that it wasn't uncommon for a mare to foal unexpectedly. She had lived in the fort all her life and, being obsessed with horses, she had spent all her spare time in the stables. She knew them all by name and character and had soaked up knowledge from the old army horsemaster. She knew far more now than any devil-may-care soldier and far more than Theo, who only knew how to ride. His slaves cared for his mare. The soldiers had the privilege (Minna thought it a privilege) of sleeping beside their horses in the stables. Not Theodosius, of course – being the commander of eighty men he had his own house and slaves to wait on him. But that didn't make him any less stupid, Minna thought, not heeding what she had told him.

Minna longed to own a pony, but knew it would never happen, not to her. The family owned two oxen, which they used to till a small piece of land her father had inherited beyond the vicus, but they were boring animals. Nice-natured but boring. Cerdic had a hunting dog, like most boys. They ganged up and took their dogs into the forest to flush out deer and boar which they tried to spear, mostly unsuccessfully. It was a red letter day when they actually came back with a warm carcass. But Minna had nothing. I want this foal! she thought.

"The centurion will want his mare back," Stuf said. "Drink up, little foal. It's probably your only chance."

Not if I get my way! thought Minna.

"I'll keep the mare in here until they come back," Minna said. "I'll hide her."

"Not for long. Everyone knows what's happened."

Stuf went off, laughing. The foal was standing now on its own but, full of milk, it soon gently collapsed at the mare's feet. Pesrut started licking him all over. Minna took off her saddle and bridle and started to brush away the sweat, smoothing the dark chestnut coat. The pony's name meant "red cloak". She was a cut above most of the cavalry animals, clearly with blood in her from the horses imported from the same country as their dark-skinned riders. Most of the ponies were native Britons, many from the North by the wall Hadrian built, bigger than southern ponies, rough things but very strong. But Pesrut had the pretty head and large lustrous eyes of the hot-blooded foreign horses. Perhaps her skinny little foal would take her beauty to add it to its willing heart, and become a great horse!

For Minna knew now that it would live.

II

Of course there was a row with Theo.

He was the centurion with men and slaves at his command, but Minna was a self-willed little girl who was the blacksmith's daughter, part of the fabric, not under his command at all. The inside of the fort was virtually a town, full of barracks, stables, dwellings, workshops, granaries: a mix of military and general business. The Roman army mixed freely with the local people. Over many years they had become one community. The native Britons had learned the Roman language Latin; the army – most of them – could converse in the local Celtic lingo as well as in Latin (and in their various outlandish tongues).

When the patrol came home Theo was riding a tall black pony, rather hairier than Pesrut but handsome all the same. It was just going dark, late – for it was May; Minna watched them come in, standing hidden just inside the gateway. Eighty ponies made a great clatter going up the street to the barracks at the far end of the fort. Theo rode, very upright in his proud, commanding way, at their head and Minna half expected him to see her and shout to her to explain her part in the day's adventure, but he went on, unseeing. From his angry expression, she guessed that he knew his misadventure had been broadcast all over the place and had caused a good deal of amusement. The centurion being tossed from his horse! Everyone was laughing. There were no secrets in this small, isolated community.

The fort was miles from anywhere, answerable mainly to the sea, which was full of threats these days. Once it had welcomed ships full of wine and gold bracelets and rare spices, but now it was more likely to be pirates from Saxony. The soldiers on lookout were rarely stood down. Theo got itchy when they reported

suspicious-looking ships. So far none had sailed in, only passed by. Minna did not like the thought of Theo leading hand-to-hand fighting, boarding a pirate ship, for all that his swordplay in sport was so impressive. When strange ships were in the offing he sent slaves off pretending to fish, to do some spying. Cerdic had gone once, dying for some excitement, but they had only found a Gaulish trader, half sunk, bailing furiously, trying to find shallow water in which to ground.

But her father said, "Aye, they'll come one day, these Saxon adventurers, and take us. Rome is finished now, since Constantine moved East to Byzantium and made it his capital. A great man, but now he's dead we're left at the mercy of any gang of scaramouches from anywhere in Europe."

"Oh come on, half your scaramouches are in the Roman army anyway," said Minna's mother. "Our own Theodosius is – well, what is he? An Egyptian? His mother was a Roman but that father of his was no more a Roman than you are. Theodosius speaks Greek like a native, as well as his own language, which certainly isn't Latin. The whole of Europe is a mix, and Britain too. We're none of us pure-bred Celts any

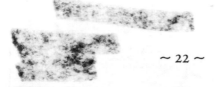

more. Your grandmother was Roman, so was my great-grandfather. And on my mother's side we are from Germania and Belgica. What is a true Briton any more?"

"Everyone looking for a better place. It's natural."

Theo's early childhood home was in Rome and when his father died his mother and siblings had gone back there. But Theo, the eldest son, had stayed, aware that he had more chance of promotion where he was than in the melting pot that was Rome. He longed to go north where the fighting was.

"Those wild men across Hadrian's Wall! There's real war up there, something to get the blood up. Nothing ever happens down here."

Minna dreaded him being drafted. Every time the tribune came on a visit Theo put his plea. But so far he was too young.

Now his pony had thrown him and galloped off home and everyone was sniggering. Minna had the mare hidden still in the hut, canoodling over her foal, and that was where she was determined she would stay.

Theo found out, naturally. He came storming down to their house, shouting for Minna. Her mother pretended to concentrate on tidying the used tableware.

Her father was out playing dice in the wine-shop, luckily.

"They say you've taken my mare," he fumed. "I want her back."

"I've looked after her. She was in a distressed state. You must have known she'd foaled?"

He was so fine in a temper, his black eyes flashing, his dark hair tossing back from his sweaty skull. He was muddy and tired, on his way to the bathhouse, his slave hovering in the street waiting to attend him. Minna wished she had the slave's job, to cosset the hard, slender body, to wait on his needs, to sleep on guard outside his room. She adored Theo. But when he pulled rank she was careful; for all they had played together as children, she knew that he had the power now to humiliate her if he wanted.

"The foal was rubbish. I told them to throw it out. She tricked us, foaling like that. She'd shown no sign. I want a cavalry horse, not a brood mare. As long as I have her back, I'll not blame you for anything."

"She's in our shelter. Come and see her. Her foal has a brave heart, to live after that treatment."

Theo groaned. "You've saved the foal?" He swore on his Roman gods, then laughed. "You women! I can't cope with your thinking! I'll get cleaned and fed and I'll sort you out tomorrow when my head is clear. At least my mare is safe, for which I thank you."

Minna walked with him as far as the bathhouse, which lay on the outside wall of the fort. Steam curled up out of the vents, along with the shouting and singing of the relaxing soldiers. Slaves were keeping the boilers well fed with fuel so that inside the building the hot-water pipes were scalding. The men sat sweating like pigs and scraping the dirt and sweat away with scraping tools. They loved the conviviality of the bathhouse, something Minna scorned. Women were allowed to use it in the mornings, but in summer Minna preferred to swim privately in one of the creeks that scored the shoreline. The bathhouse was all right in the winter, of course, but the heat made one dozy, loathe to come out. The plunge bath at the end cured that, cold as ice.

"Thank the gods for bathhouses!"

Theo's bad temper was receding as he could now look forward to being cosseted and massaged and perfumed and made like new after the hard day's excursion, and Minna gave him a grateful smile as she parted from him. Whatever his humour she never tired of being in his company, watching the expressions chase over his volatile face. She was aware that he regarded her slightly differently these days, now that she was eleven, no longer a child. She thought maybe he liked the look of her, for her mother told her she was pretty and had held up a polished silver tray to try to show her her reflection. But she wasn't a simpering, flirting sort of girl so, beyond washing her hair more often and dressing a little more carefully, she just had to hope that Theo would prefer her to some of the others. He certainly had plenty of admirers, amongst the older women too. Minna dreamed her dreams, enmeshed in the claustrophobic life of the fort, which buzzed like a beehive on the lip of the sea.

Away from the crowd, making for her hut out in the fields, she lifted her face gratefully to the silent sky. What a blessing that she had the old place to retreat to, crouched on the edge of the forest! She loved the silence, the great spread of the marshes stretching to the sea and the horizon on one side, and on the other, inland, the dark forest. A clear night, the sky was bright with stars. The air smelled of sea-wrack and trodden earth and salty decaying things left by the tide. And over all the smell of spring coming. Minna's heart gave a leap of happiness. How lucky she was!

She would persuade Theo tomorrow, she was convinced, to do what she wanted. She would *beguile* him! She laughed out loud.

She went into the hut, ducking through the doorway, and found the little chestnut mare lying down beside her foal. The foal slept, breathing steadily. Minna crept in and lay down beside it, pulling a blanket over both of them, and the three of them slept together.

III

Theodosius Valerian Aquila – to give him his full name – knew in his heart that he was going to give way to that little Celtic firebrand Minna. Once she wanted something she nearly always got it, and she wanted his mare. What a pity she wasn't a boy! The army needed firebrands. Sometimes he despaired of the men he worked with, a motley bunch bored by life in this backwater of Roman civilization. As was he. It was a quiet life in the Othona fort. What was the use of being a soldier if there was no one to fight? It was quiet in Essex, no uprisings anywhere. And their fort was miles from any proper road and passing traffic. The only threat came from the sea and lately all had been serene out there.

These thoughts were in his head as he stalked out of the gate towards Minna's family hut. His parents hadn't mixed much during their life in the fort, only with the other army inhabitants. But as a child Theo had been drawn into friendships with the scruffy native population, boys like Cerdic particularly. The native boys did not have to slave at lessons all day and sit politely at long, political meetings with the tribune. They roamed freely over the marshes and forest, chasing boar, fishing, gathering firewood, laughing and shouting. Of course they worked too, right from an early age, helping their parents: some were worked as hard as the Roman slaves and beaten too, but they had none of the army ethic to weigh them down. Theo was steeped in army tradition.

Which was why he found it difficult to cope with Minna, who answered only to her parents. Her parents were dependent on the army for their living and would beat their children if they did not respect army rules in the fort, but unfortunately Minna still saw Theo more as a playmate than a newly raised – if temporary – commander. She would not do as she was told! Not what he told her, at least.

When he entered the dark hovel he found Minna sitting in the straw beside the sleeping foal. The mare Pesrut was calmly eating a bundle of reeds Minna had given her, but put back her ears at the sight of Theo and moved to stand protectively over her foal.

"See, she hates you for being so cruel," Minna said.

The girl did not even stand up respectfully, but attacked like a little cat. She knew that Theo was refreshed now, ready for an argument.

"She has a job to do. How can I operate without a mount?"

"Find another. That was a good one you came home on."

"That is Hilarion's. I borrowed it for the day. I'm not given to stealing other people's possessions."

"It isn't Hilarion's. It belongs to the Roman army, like Pesrut here. Not to you."

By the gods, she was sharp!

"She is in my care," he said.

That was the wrong remark to make.

"Care! You call that care, how you treated her? That's fine!" Very sarcastic.

Theo, although needled by her words, could not help admiring the fire in the little white face that stared up at him. The sea-green eyes spat scorn. He had to laugh, which was wrong again.

"You don't care! You're just like Cerdic! The Roman army *needs* horses, and you just throw them away. This little foal has the heart of a lion. It—"

"It's rubbish and you know it. It's kinder to kill it."

"Its body is puny, yes, but it has such a will to live. Such a heart. That is what you need in battle, isn't it? Of course it's puny, the way you used the mare all the while she was in foal. You have no sense!"

"She never had access to a stallion. She conceived by magic. How was I to know she was in foal?"

"Don't talk rubbish. Eleven months ago a shipment of Barbary horses was landed here. I have been thinking about it. Don't you remember? And Pesrut was in the fields out of the way and the Barbary horses were put in a corral until the next morning. I'll bet that's where the sire came from, from the Barbarys in the corral. You took them away the next morning, to deliver them to the mansio in Caesaromagus. And Pesrut was left pregnant."

"Could be, yes. I remember the Barbary horses.

In that case you are right, it might be a nice animal."

Minna beamed. Theo laughed. What was the point of challenging good sense?

"Then you'll rear this little thing to be my next mount? Half Barbary, half Pesrut, who is a native and sensible as any horse can be – a good prospect."

Minna looked worried. "Cerdic has laid claim to it."

"Cerdic?"

"I had to get him to help me. And he said yes if it could be his, when it was ready to ride."

"Well, we'll quarrel about that later. But yes, you can keep Pesrut until the foal is weaned. And weaned early, I insist. Three months."

"Four months," she challenged. He knew she wanted six.

"Three months." He was curt now, having given way so easily. What sort of a commander was he going to make, to be talked down by a little girl?

But as she got to her feet he saw that she wasn't a little girl any longer. He knew why he gave way, because he saw in her the young woman she was going to be in another year or two, strong and beautiful. Her face glowed with victory. He could not begrudge it.

He left her abruptly, turning his mind back to the duties that the day demanded.

Minna watched him go, loving the arrogance of his bearing, the grace of his step. She had won and he hadn't been too cross. If he laid claim to the foal it would be difficult after her promise to Cerdic. But there was plenty of time to sort that out. Whatever they decided, she knew that the foal was *hers*. By the time it was ready to ride three years would have passed, and during that time only she would care for it. It would know her for ever. Let them claim what they liked. The little foal was hers!

IV

After losing his foal coat Minna's treasure grew a dark smooth coat of an unusual bluish-black.

"So, he is going to be a grey. More Barbary than native," Theo remarked dubiously.

Greys, when they inevitably grew lighter in colour with age, showed up in the dark, not good when out on marauding patrol.

"Maybe you won't want him then?"

Theo laughed. "But maybe I will! He's extremely handsome for a youngster, I have to admit. He will set me off nicely."

"Oh, you're so vain!" But with such good reason, Minna knew! Of course she would not pay him any compliments. But her eyes loved him.

"Anyway, he's Cerdic's," she said.

"Cerdic likes dogs better than horses. That bitch of his never leaves his side."

"Yes, he dotes on her. But he thinks Silva is his."

"Silva?"

"That's his name."

Minna had christened the foal after Silvanus, the god of wild things.

After its initial weakness the foal had thrived. Its frame was never going to be as big as Theo would wish, but it was very well put together: deep through the girth, short-backed, with a well-set neck. And its head had the lovely shape of the hot-blooded Arab, wide between the eyes and with a delicate muzzle and large nostrils. Its eyes were large and enquiring. There was no more handsome animal in the fort, Minna knew. By comparison, the rest were all common.

By the time he was a yearling and had shed his winter coat, Silva was a dark steel grey. He answered to Minna's devotion and would follow her about like a dog. He understood her voice commands. This was because Minna had spent so much time with him. She took her work out to the hut and did it there with Silva for company, talking to him all the while. She helped her mother in sewing the soldiers' tunics and their leather jerkins, and spinning the rough wool to make the tunics. The work was never-ending. The only job she really enjoyed was putting the finishing embroidery to a new toga for Theo, to wear when the tribune came.

The tribune, the ruler of the city of Camulodunum from which they were commanded, had still not decided who would officially command Othona. Theo had carried on where his father had left off, but there were several jealous men who thought they should be commander of the fort. One was a long-serving Roman called Octavius who expected to be promoted as soon as the rather absent-minded tribune Tiberius got round to making the command official. Octavius found it hard to take orders from someone he thought was just a boy. Theo had the intelligence to understand this.

One day in the spring of the following year this relationship was put to the test.

It was Minna who gave the alarm, her hawk eyes

seeing what the lazy lookouts on the ramparts failed to notice. She had been for a swim, far out over the saltings where the soldiers could not see her. The sea came to the land via a myriad of small deep creeks where the water was warm and quiet, swelling gently on the tide. On a summer's day it was bliss to lie floating, looking up at the white rags of seagulls gliding on the faintest of zephyrs far above, listening to the cry of the curlews over the marsh. How any woman could prefer the bathhouse to the sea in summer she could not understand. But most women did not roam the marshes and saltings as she did, afraid of getting stuck in a bog. Minna knew her way over the land like a wild cat. She and Cerdic had played all their lives in the creeks, making dams and make-believe harbours, and boats out of twigs which they raced, and covering each other with mud for fun. In those days Theo had joined them in their larks. But now only Minna came, and Cerdic sometimes to fish. Their playing days were over.

The shallow, treacherous sea was blue for once, rather than tawny-brown as it usually was. Unmarked sandbanks far out caught foreign ships unawares and wrecked many. There was a ship out there now. It did not look like the usual trading ship to Minna, although she could not have said exactly why. Something about the rig and sails told her it was foreign. And, by the shape of it, it was built for speed, not for carrying goods.

Othona fort had been built over a hundred years ago to withstand foreign pirates, along with several others round the southern shores. The forts were strong and forbidding enough to deter attack, and guarded the shore well, sending out forays to fight the pirates that came from the North to sniff out likely landing places for a swift raid, or plunder the Roman merchant ships that plied the coast. This ship was unlikely to attack the fort, but Minna suspected they were marauders looking to plunder passing vessels offshore. Trading ships from the Mediterranean carrying valuable materials were poorly armed and made rich pickings for pirates. Othona was well-placed to intercept pirates.

Minna scrambled out of the sea and into her clothes, still wet, and ran for home. The lookouts had only just noticed the ship and obviously thought it was local. The clods! They had not even called the commander.

Minna interrupted him in the forum, talking to Octavius.

"There's a foreign ship offshore. I think it's pirates!"

"By Jupiter, girl, who do you think you're talking to?" Octavius barked.

"Minna, have respect!" Theo said sharply.

But she knew that, unlike Octavius, he took notice of what she said.

He said to Octavius, "The girl has eyes like a hunting bird. She could be right. Shall we go and look?"

A question, not a command. Octavius might be an experienced soldier, but he had no graces, no tact, like Theo. Theo was a natural leader, and perhaps it was for this reason that the tribune, recognizing the fact, had not yet put Octavius above him.

"Leave us, Minna," Theo said to her sharply.

Minna watched them walk – quite quickly – to the steps that led up to the ramparts. The lookouts fell back to attention. Minna would have followed but for Theo's rebuke.

"You don't know your place, Minna!" her mother said to her sharply, having watched the incident from where she was delivering new tunics to the quartermaster. "Get about your work. Theo isn't your playmate any more. Remember that!"

"No." Minna smiled. He was her love – not that her mother didn't recognize the fact.

"You have ideas above your station," her mother said. "Keep your love for that horse."

They both laughed.

"There's pirates out there. I just told him. He'll be pleased I saw them."

She watched Theo and Octavius up on the ramparts, taking in the situation. Although she could not hear their words she knew exactly how the conversation was going.

"Let him pass by. The garrison in the Colne can deal with him." Cautious Octavius never went looking for trouble, although he quelled it efficiently enough when it came his way.

Impetuous Theo wanted action. "If we launch at once we can catch him. The wind is on our beam. We can at least head him off for home. And if we board him, who knows what treasure he's got on board?"

Minna could see the excitement in his stance.

"I don't advise it," Octavius was muttering. Theo came flying down the steps, shouting orders. His slave came running with his breastplate and sword; the men on the quay swarmed to get the fast interceptor ship ready to sail. It all happened very quickly. Minna was thrilled momentarily with what she had set in action, then cold fear clutched at her when she saw Theo armed for fighting.

Octavius was right: let the ship pass by, live in peace! The fort was in an uproar.

"You're in charge here, Octavius, and will remain so if I don't come back. We'll part with goodwill, eh?" Theo turned back briefly to the older man.

They clasped hands, and then Theo was running down to the quay, his picked bodyguard already aboard the fast fighting ship, the *Othona*, that was the pride of the fort. They were archers and swordsmen of the greatest skill, well-trained by Theo in constant drills and practice. Theo, unlike Octavius, rarely spent a day in repose.

Minna watched with her mother, miserable now.

"He might get killed," Minna whispered.

"It's his job. He's right to go. Jupiter will protect him."

Cerdic came up to them, his dog at his heels.

"How I wish I was with him! He should have taken

me – I know the shoals out there better than those so-called sailors of his! I bet they'll put him aground before he catches up with them!"

"Oh come, big-head!" His mother put her arm affectionately round his shoulders. "You're only fourteen. The Roman army doesn't take children. You'll be with them soon enough."

His mother didn't want Cerdic to join the army. She wanted him to follow his father in the blacksmith's shop, making armour and swords and horseshoes. It was a good trade, never wanting for work.

Now, Minna found it hard to go back to her chores. The boat, named *Othona* after the fort, was already winging out from the shore and everyone thronged out onto the quay to watch her progress. Luckily the tide was well enough up for her to be free from the shallows. She was not large, carrying about twenty soldiers, and was built narrower than the cumbersome merchant ships. She could be rowed in light or unfair winds, but the oars were not needed now. A bone of white water creamed under her bows as she heeled to the wind. The soldiers sat out on her windward side to balance her. Minna saw Theo order them, standing on the sternboard beside the rudder man. He already had his sword unsheathed as if he could not wait. But Minna knew boarding was a dangerous business. The pirate ship would be armed and waiting, their swords as quick, their lives at stake. It had gone about, to flee for home, but the *Othona* was closing fast.

"We shan't see what happens. They'll be too far away," Cerdic complained.

Minna started to tremble. She wondered why she had raised the alarm; why hadn't she let the pirate ship sail quietly by? If Theo was killed, it would be her own fault! How could she be such a fool?

The same thought was lingering at the back of Theo's mind too, as he took in the strength of the ship they were fast approaching. The crew, he could see, were falling over themselves to get armed rather than bother about sailing the ship to her best advantage, so it was clear that battle was not going to be avoided. Unless they capitulated. Doubtful. He could see that their numbers were roughly similar to his own, and these men lived by killing. His own men had never yet been in a real fight, and nor had he. If he bungled it, he would lose his post. Octavius would say he had advised against the action. As indeed he had.

Theo's brain told him all this but his instinct was raring to go. His men, too, he could see were excited, joking to cover up fear, a few sending up prayers to Mithras and Jupiter and their own motley gods. They were all young and keen: Theo hadn't wanted old soldiers in his bodyguard, however battle-hardened. He wanted hot young blood like his own.

"Arm your bows!" he ordered.

A shower of arrows once within range should thin them out.

The crew of *Othona* was standing by to drop sail and man the grapnels. The enemy had left their ship to her own devices while they armed and she wallowed up to wind, a sitting duck. Her sailors were a hideous-looking crew, filthy and unshaven, shouting excitedly in a guttural Northern tongue. But their swords were clean and shining and sparkled in the May sun.

Theo sent up a prayer to Mithras and for a fleeting moment thought of the comforts of his life in the fort, of his devoted slave and the flashing eyes of that funny little Minna – how crazy! He shouted: "Fire!" and a shower of arrows whistled like a flock of birds through the sky. Considering the motion of the ship the firing was accurate. The pirate ship was about fifty metres away and several of the men nearest the gunwale were hit. A ghastly screaming went up and there was a great scramble to pull the injured away. In the chaos two bodies were flung over the side with scarcely time to die.

"Prepare to board!"

The pirates were yelling and leaping about like madmen but Theo's men stood like statues, swords at the ready, as the grapnels swung. The sharp points of the heavy metal bedded over the gunwale with satisfying clunks, impossible to pull free as the ropes came taut and the two ships crashed violently together. Theo kept his feet and ran down from the stern to athwartships, jumped up onto the rail and bawled at this men: "Aboard! Aboard!" He was the leader, first up and over.

So this was battle! He scarcely knew what he was doing, save that his hours of sword practice guided his flailing arm. The Roman swords were flat and broad, built for close-quarters to hack and thrust, easy to pull out and thrust again. The pirates wore no breastmail, only leather, and old at that, giving no protection. Theo's sword plunged eagerly and pirate blood sprayed into his face, hot and thick. He smelled the panting breath, got a mouthful of stinking hair and parried upward to the throat as he had been taught, half severing the ugly head that leered down at him. The eyes went suddenly blank. Theo felt a great burning pain somewhere down his side but it did not stop him as he spun to deflect a sparkling iron blade about to behead him in its turn. He struck it so hard that it flew out of its wielder's hand and into the sea. The swordsman gave a roar like an injured boar and flung his whole body at Theo, smashing him to the deck. He had fists like battering rams but as he raised them young Flavius stabbed him in the back and he fell on Theo like a sack of corn. Flavius kicked him off and held out his hand.

"You're hurt!"

"No."

Theo could not feel it. But as Flavius stood before him, getting his breath, the flash of a blade in the sunlight exploded suddenly behind his head and instinct brought Theo's sword up to parry it. The accompanying stab of pain in his side made Theo cry out, but the clash of colliding metal was fierce enough: Flavius ducked, spun round and was in time to see the enemy sword, successfully deflected, spin harmlessly across the deck. Unarmed, the pirate stood – fatally – gawping and Flavius thrust him in the midriff. Theo managed to turn his unseemly cry of agony into a shout of victory as the man buckled up at his feet, and he finished him off with a blow across the back of his neck. How easy it was to kill or be killed! The man's hand was groping desperately for his sword even as he gasped his last breath.

"I owed you that, Flavius!"

There was time, suddenly, for a heartfelt embrace. A momentary, instinctive gesture, then Theo, with Flavius guarding him, was able to take stock, lowering his sword. His men had done well for, like himself, they were standing back, reviewing the obviously successful attack, guarding the writhing, swearing, mangled remains of the pirates. Some of the enemy had jumped overboard and were swimming away, some were floating bodies, most were lying on deck, vanquished, many badly wounded and several dead. It had been quick and incredibly violent. Theo felt incredulous. Was it over already? He was still panting, and suddenly sickened by a glimpse of the man he had half-beheaded. The whole sea and sky suddenly seemed to be turning over and changing places. He staggered, and then jerked himself up – he was in charge! Weakness was not an option.

"Get the dead overboard!" His voice rang out harshly. "Chain up the prisoners."

The training which he had had drummed painfully into him all his life mercifully came to his aid. He knew what was to be done. The pirates were a cunning lot: the wounded could still kill if backs were turned. After a quick inspection, he had the worst cases thrown overboard and the rest bound tightly and chained to the gunwales. Once that danger was overcome there were his own wounded to attend to: not many, luckily, and only one dead, a good man whose courage had never been in doubt. He had been stabbed in the back, no doubt when killing someone else. One needed luck as well as skill in fighting! The body was laid out reverently and covered with a bit of tattered sailcloth. The sight of so much blood was unnerving Theo, who was aware of losing quite a lot of his own as he picked his way over the slippery deck. But the one skilled medical man in his band he instructed to tend to his soldiers: he would rather die than seek aid before his men. The others, ecstatic in their victory, were quickly put to work: manning the pirate ship to get it back to the fort. But first Theo wanted to explore what possible booty it held. His bad luck if they were fresh out and had not yet captured anything!

The pirate ship was open, with only a small cuddy in the bows, covered with leather skins. Theo went to look; Flavius went with him. Under the skins were several wooden chests. They were locked.

"Get them open," Theo ordered.

He was beginning to feel dangerously weak, and did not want to waste time. Whatever wound he had suffered, it was no mere scratch. The sooner they got home the better. But if the chests held booty, they would sail with better heart.

Flavius hacked furiously at the boxes with his bloody sword and Theo's spirits lifted immediately at the sight of what lay within. Yes, the pirates had had rich pickings, mostly in jewellery and gold. One chest in particular held some exquisite tableware and a set of silver chalices. There was a lot of rubbish as well, in the way of skins of leather and fleeces and dried meat and carving tools, useful but not valuable. But the jewellery–! Theo called the men to take a look. It would cheer them up, for they only had wounds to prize so far.

"It shall be fairly shared, if we are allowed," Theo said. "I promise you."

If Octavius stolidly reported to the tribune, as was very likely, the best of it would be taken from them. Theo would fight to avoid that. His men had fought like wild boars, why should they not have their reward? For many of them, like himself, it was their first taste of real battle and the promise of a prize would counteract the shaky, nauseous feelings that now assailed them. They were quiet now, their euphoria damped by the moans of the injured. But the glint of gold gave them heart.

The beam wind that had served them on the way out served now to see them home. His sailors got the pirate ship's sails drawing to best advantage. She was no slouch sailed properly, and kept up with their own *Othona*, now manned by a skeleton crew. Theo could make out the low-lying shore of their home ahead of them, as well as the slightly nearer mouth of the river that led to Camulodunum. They should be well pleased with him there!

The sun shone serenely and the birds went about

their way as if no life was at stake, no deaths recently bloodying the waters below. They drifted across a sky of softest blue. How great to be alive! Theo thought with a shiver. Reaction was setting in. He yearned for the sanctuary of the fort. His men were half laughing, half trembling and he was losing his strength fast. But he forced himself to stay standing by the helmsman as they dipped through the bright sea. He could feel the warm blood oozing down his side. It trickled down his bare leg and into his sandal and the men saw it but no one dared say anything. Only Flavius stood anxiously by him.

"Our medics will have plenty on their hands," he said.

"We have our reward. Octavius cannot complain."

If they had been defeated... Theo did not care to think about it. He had acted impetuously, he knew. The pirates were a far more battle-hardened bunch than his own picked men. But the battle will have blooded his men. They needed reality. As he did too. The satisfaction of victory against the odds warmed him, even though he felt faint. The looming shoreline danced before his eyes. He had done well and must see it out. He took a strong hold on his failing senses and was still standing erect and proud as the soldiers in the fort swarmed out to greet them. Even Octavius was smiling.

The day was good.

V

Minna pushed her way up onto the ramparts to get a view of the pirate ship's arrival. Octavius and his men were on the quay and she would get short shrift if she ventured down there. But her heart was hammering in her chest with fear until she saw that the man standing in the stern of the captured ship was Theo. Then the sweep of relief was so sweet she laughed out loud.

"Oh, he's safe! He's safe!"

Her mother was not impressed.

"Not like some. That's a fair day's killing." Her lips formed private prayers for the dead, to the god she favoured. Life was short and brutal, she well knew, but Othona was a relatively peaceful station. Mutilated bodies were a rare sight.

"Come away," she said to Minna. "We can help later, if there's nursing to do."

Octavius was ordering the getting ashore of the wounded and the rounding up of the captured men. Theo had no more to do. He came ashore to meet Octavius, but weakness made him stumble. The mission accomplished, will power was no longer enough to sustain him. Octavius caught him, swearing softly.

"You're hurt! But a successful attack – I was wrong, Theodosius. I salute you."

"See to the booty – there's rich pickings for us all," Theo murmured. The pain in his side was like fire, he could say no more. His men carried him away to his house, where Minna was barred admittance. His servants laughed at her and shooed her away.

"Come away. Have you no pride?" her mother said angrily, and dragged her home.

"He might die!"

"So might we all."

She was set to work on thonging leather jerkins, but found it hard to ignore the excitement of the day.

Cerdic came running in with news of the treasure, of the gruesome wounds, the keening of the women over the dead soldier, the glitter of gold in the wooden chests. Why was he never set jobs to do as she was? Minna wondered. Just waiting to join the army, he spent his time doing as he pleased. He hung around the soldiers all day, unless he was out fishing or hunting with his dog.

His dog was a very fine wolfhound bitch called Mel. He wanted to find a suitable mate for her to breed a valuable litter: well-bred hunting dogs fetched a good price.

"It's all you think about, your silly dog," Minna often complained.

"And all you think about, *my* horse! Wait till it's old enough to ride. We'll see whose it is then."

Minna hated Cerdic then, always laying claim to her beloved Silva because of the rash promise she had made. Surely he would not hold her to it when the time came? She would do all the training, Cerdic was far too lazy. And if Silva turned out as beautiful as she guessed he would, who knew that Theo might claim him? And she would have no answer to that. The injustice choked her.

"It's not fair," she complained to her mother, stitching angrily at the tough leather. "Cerdic does nothing but play about."

"Life's not fair, Minna."

"Go and find out how Theo is, how badly he is hurt," Minna ordered Cerdic. "You've nothing else to do, and I need to know. Ask Benoc."

Benoc was Theo's slave, a Roman youth who had been sold into slavery by his parents. He had stayed with Theo when the household moved back to Rome. Minna was jealous of him, so close to Theo. She would be Theo's slave, if she could. (Save she knew it was not in her nature to be a slave.) She was worried now about Theo, although her mother assured her that his wound could not be too serious if he had stayed on his feet long enough to sail to shore. But Minna knew that wounds often went bad, and could kill days or even weeks later.

"He is in the best hands," her mother said. "They will make sure he doesn't die."

"I thought the gods decided," Minna said slyly. It was what her mother often said to her.

"They decide in the end, that's true. You must say your prayers."

But Minna had never really decided which of the many gods would listen to anything she had to say, whether the gods of war – Mars, Jupiter, Juno, Mithras and so on – were of more use than her mother's homely trust in Ceres, the earth goddess. She preferred Silvanus, god of the wild, after whom she had christened her horse. Pray to the sky, the sun, the clouds and birds and the beauty of the forests and marshes...that was how she felt praying worked best, when she was happy and wanted to sing. But to pray to save Theo – she was at a loss. He had told her that he was going to become a Christian because it was a good career move. He hadn't much idea what Christianity was, but it helped promotion if one professed an interest. It was a newish religion, from the East. It believed in love, apparently, which made a change. If Theo became a Christian, he would love her! So Minna prayed as she sewed, for Theo not to die.

Theo was very fit and healthy, but he had suffered a deep wound just above the hip and lost a lot of blood. By the time it had been cleaned and sewed up he was barely conscious and very weak. He lay on a couch hallucinating, seeing the grinning head that he had all but cut off, coming and going in his vision. Once or twice he cried out. He had never killed before. Benoc sat by him, bathing his hot brow, changing the blood-soaked sheet, offering drinks of water.

It wasn't that he wasn't familiar with violence: he had ridden many times with his father, seen his father kill recalcitrant Britons, even a spying, lying Roman on one occasion. He knew the savage strength of the sword. But he had never used his own before in earnest, taking a life to save his own. He was ashamed of dwelling on it, like a girl, not being able to shrug it off. He was a soldier, wasn't he? It was all in a day's work.

When, in the evening, Benoc reported that "that wretched little girl Minna is at the door", Theo muttered, "Bring her in." To Minna he could boast of the day's doings without fear of contradiction. It would make him feel better. He was a hero after all. Why could he not feel like one? At least he was to Minna.

"Leave us, Benoc."

Benoc scowled but backed off.

Minna could not believe her luck, given access. Theo's house was heated under the floor by the hypocaust and on this cool spring evening the luxury of the warmth under her bare feet on the patterned tiles was gorgeous. Theo lay on his good side, propped on pillows, his shoulders bare, the swathing of bandages showing above the embroidered rugs that covered the rest of him. Minna dropped down beside him and the look of adoration on her face made him laugh. But laughing hurt.

"There, I'm still alive. You're pleased?"

"Oh, of course I am! I was so afraid for you. They'd have sailed past and no harm done if I hadn't called to you."

"Yes, but it was good, Minna. You should see the stuff we've captured! I will make sure that you have a reward. I will choose you a piece of jewellery, Minna, that will make you happy, believe me."

His black eyes gleamed with pride in the soft light from the oil lamp, but Minna could see the gaunt hollows of pain in his cheeks. Beads of sweat stood out on his brow and his hair clung damply to his skull. She could tell he was feverish and his condition could well be dangerous.

"You must be well looked after. My mother will come, if you want. She is a good nurse."

"Benoc is good. I just need to rest a day or two."

"I will nurse you!"

"No, you make me feverish, Minna. I want a calming presence." He laughed again, grimaced with the pain. "I am all stitched up like a porker full of stuffing. It hurts to talk to you, Minna. Come tomorrow, I shall be better."

She could see that he was speaking the truth. The sword thrust was deep and painful and he was scared to move.

"Do you have a sleeping potion? My mother can get one for you."

"No. Benoc has all I need."

Already he was drifting off again, his small reserve of energy exhausted. Minna sat beside him while he slipped away into unconsciousness. She stayed on, watching over him, while the sky deepened in the courtyard outside and lit its stars one by one. The night was clear and the sky glittered from horizon to horizon. Minna lifted her face to it and prayed to the new god Jesus, if that was the one that would do Theo the most good.

"Look after him. Don't let him die," she ordered. And then a prayer to Silvanus and Ceres and Jupiter for good measure.

Perhaps Benoc was more use, though, than any of these. He came up silently, to watch through the night. He was like a girl, Minna thought, with his dark red hair and curious black, almond-shaped eyes. Minna knew he hated her. Did he suspect Theo loved her, was he jealous? Did Theo love her? He never made it known, with his teasing, his lies. But he was to give her a jewel, a ring perhaps, a promise? Minna shivered with delight.

She got up to take her leave. "Look after him," she said to Benoc.

"I always do, without your telling me."

That was as rude as a slave dared, Minna guessed, but she did not take it amiss. She could order him to be flogged if she wished, and he knew it. Theo had him flogged if he was in a bad temper. The life of a slave, even a favoured one, was hard.

I will have a slave when I'm old and rich, Minna promised herself. She wanted a warm floor under her feet and hangings of rich brocade on her walls like Theo's. As it was, she went out of the fort, slipping past the sentries into the sweet-smelling spring night.

"Going to sleep with 'er 'orse," said the sentry with a guffaw.

"Aye, she's a weird one. A bit of magic in her, I reckon."

"Takes all sorts."

Silva, loose in the hut, came to meet Minna with a soft fluttering of welcome in his nostrils.

"My lovely boy," Minna whispered. "I love you too, you know. After Theo, I love you best. Whatever happens, you will always be mine, won't you? Mine really, even if others take you."

That was more than you could say for a man. She knew that.

VI

By the time he was a yearling Silva was undeniably a striking colt. Everyone save Minna and Cerdic had forgotten that he had been thrown out at birth. Now all was admiration. He was perfectly proportioned and had the quality of the Eastern horse that most of the hairy beasts in the fort lacked. Not that the hairy beasts lacked courage and endurance, but in their looks they could not hold a candle to Silva. They came mostly from the hills and moors of the North and West where they lived in the wild, and were incredibly strong for their size.

Silva, with his devoted upbringing, was tame and gentle. He understood Minna's words of command and would stay if she asked it, move on when commanded, come to a whistle. Minna longed for the day when she could see him gallop but for now there was no open field to put him in. He had to go with the oxen, who were contained by a mere ditch and bank, which Silva could have pranced over without effort. He had to be tethered or hobbled, for the fresh grass tempted him. Minna often led him out where it was best and sat by him while he grazed. Of course her mother made her take work with her, sewing the interminable rough woollen tunics the soldiers wore. The material came in ships from Norfolk where the sheep were raised.

"You are a lucky beast, Silva, having no work to do. Not yet."

He would be three before he was ready to ride. By then Minna would be fourteen, Cerdic seventeen and Theo twenty. They all wanted Silva. Minna lifted her chin at the thought. Cerdic would be in the army by then and she knew he wanted Silva as his mount and to keep him in the horse barracks in the fort. The soldiers slept by their horses and tended them well, but Minna could not bear the thought of parting with him. And yet she accepted the truth of Cerdic's jibe.

"You just want him for a pet! What sort of a horse is that?"

It was true. He was too good not to work. If she had to lose him, it would be better if Theo had him and he would lead the troop under the legion standard, the magnet of all eyes. That would be grand! But Theo, amazingly, acknowledged her ownership.

"I cannot believe I had him thrown out," he said. "You did well to recover him, Minna. What a waste if he had died!"

He had walked out of the fort and through the crowded vici to find Minna in the ox field with her yearling. She stood up as he approached, slowly learning the respect her mother was always insisting on. She wasn't a child any more, her mother said. And she did not want Theo to think of her as a child.

Theo was limping from his wound. It hurt him still, but he walked out to overcome what he thought of as weakness, in taking so long to recover. Minna's mother told him rest would do better, but he took no notice. He had to overcome weakness.

He sat down on the field bank where Minna's tunics were laid.

"Have you a smart one for me? The tribune is coming tomorrow."

"We have it at home. Benoc is collecting it. It is new and I have embroidered the hem myself. You will be as smart as the tribune himself."

"He's coming to reward me. All due to you, Minna, for seeing that ship was a pirate."

Minna glowed. By recognizing the pirate ship she had sent Theo to what could well have been his death. She had nearly killed him! That was forgotten now.

"I think he will give me command of the fort. Over poor old Octavius. That's what I'm hoping. And probably take away our lovely treasure."

"All of it?" Minna still had not had her promised reward.

"No. Not all. They are fair. We shall be left some. I will make sure my men get a share. They fought well."

"And you too."

"Not well enough! Not with this beastly cut. I'm like an old woman still."

"Oh, it's soon yet. At least it mended clean."

"Yes. That poor boy Antonius died of his cut, and it wasn't as deep as mine. And Lysanias is very ill, even now. Your mother is caring for him."

"I know. She sends me out to gather herbs. She does her best."

"And you have to do her work! Poor Minna."

He laughed – heartlessly, Minna thought. His soldiers, after their drills and patrols and cleaning and building jobs, had more spare time than she did, she often thought. Although at least she didn't have to work on the walls and hump stone to make roads. The walls were more than a hundred years old now and even if they were as thick at the bottom as two men laid end to end, there were always wobbly parts higher up that needed attention. The sea ate restlessly at the eastern wall when the tide was high, weakening the foundations, and the wooden quays were forever needing repair.

"We need more men here, just to keep the place in good order. But I doubt we'll get them. We're not in the battle line here."

"Why do you want more fighting?" Minna asked crossly. Why could he not be thankful for an easy berth?

"Oh, men like fighting! I'm no different. What else is there? Some boar-hunting – that's exciting. Or go to the circus and watch the gladiators, or have your horses in a chariot to race – but we have none of that out here. Nothing beats battle, surely?"

"What, and get a great wound in your side?"

"But I didn't feel it! That's the point. During battle you're living on a different plane, like you're mad – gloriously! I can't describe how it feels. I would give anything to go where there's more fighting. I'm trained for it, Minna – my father taught me right from when I was little. He had a small sword made for me and taught me how to use it. I am a good swordsman, and so are all my men. We have no need to feel afraid."

Minna did not say anything, thinking of the two who died, and the other who was likely to. Perhaps their fathers hadn't trained them with little swords. But she had to admit that ordinary work was fairly boring. Sewing tunics was stultifying. Going off to fight must stir the blood, she could see that. Othona was not a busy place and saw no passing life, out on its lonely seashore. Perhaps that was what Theo missed, not fighting for his life, but life itself.

"Why didn't you go back to Rome with your family?"

"Why, what would I do in Rome? It's all talking

there, and back-stabbing. If I get my command here, tomorrow, I shall be well pleased."

Sitting on the bank in the warm sunshine, they both were aware of the pleasure of each other's company and the moment of deep happiness. All had gone well: there was much to look forward to. There was no cloud in the sky and the sea was calm, one or two merchant ships coming south to the great river Thamesis with hardly a breeze to fill their heavy sails. No pirates. Only peace. And the horse cropping happily beside them, his dark coat shining with well-being. The rhythmic sound of his munching mingled sweetly with the shrilling of the larks over the marshes. From the encroaching forest came the distant snortling of contented pigs where a boy watched them, and a pair of buzzards soared high over all, able to see their world like a map, Minna thought. How wonderful to be up there! They could see from the great garrison at Camulodunum to the tribune's forum at Caesaromagus, even to the seething port of Londinium. And right across the sea to where the pirates came from, the cold lands of the North.

But Theo said, "Some of those pirates we captured are Romans, would you believe? Deserters from the army. Tiberius will have them killed. I left him the pleasure."

Minna shivered. Who would die, on a day like this? The men only thought of killing.

The next day, Theo had his reward. He came out (by a great effort not limping at all, Minna noticed) to meet the tribune Tiberius, who had ridden out from Caesaromagus with all his smart retinue. (Minna noticed that Tiberius's horse was not to be compared with hers.) Theo looked splendid in his white toga, his hair tidily cut, his lovely arrogant nose lifted high as he waited on the steps of the forum.

Tiberius embraced him, and they went inside to inspect the captured treasure. Octavius was with them, cold-faced. A fine banquet was spread in the atrium and they talked until well into the evening. When Tiberius departed the next day, with a train of prisoners chained between his soldiers, Theo stood at the gates in salute. Theodosius Valerian Aquila was now the proclaimed cohort commander. Tiberius had overlooked his youth. He was following in his father's footsteps – "trained from birth" – as Tiberius acknowledged. The wooden treasure chests were slung over a heavy saddle-horse.

"But he left us plenty," Theo said happily to Minna, when all was quiet again. Theo, back in his tunic and leather jerkin, now wore a heavy gold bracelet on his wrist. His men had all had a pick of the booty and were now rejoicing in the drinking house.

"And for you too, Minna, as I promised," he said. "Look."

Minna held her breath. She did not want a bracelet or necklace, only a ring.

Theo opened his hand. On his palm lay a ruby, simply mounted in gold. A ring. Its beauty lay in its simplicity. The stone was flawless and perfectly set. Minna's eyes gleamed, but it wasn't its value that thrilled her, only of what it might mean.

"A keepsake," he said.

"Keepsake?" Minna didn't know what a keepsake was.

"To remember me by."

"Why should I forget you? You're not going away?"

"No. But girls have short memories. Girls are fickle."

"I'm not. And I shall never forget you, wherever you might go."

"Well, now you won't, I'm making sure."

He smiled and Minna saw amusement in his raven-black eyes. Not really tenderness, but love of a sort. Or so she felt. It was enough. She wanted to hug and kiss him, but now he was the commander and she had learned to show respect. She shivered with pleasure. He put the ring on her finger where she had hoped it would go. It fitted perfectly.

"There. To remember me by, even when I am under your nose."

And he laughed and turned back into the fort, and Minna went away to find Silva and show him her new treasure.

VII

"Why do you have to be so rough with him? His mouth is like silk!"

Minna stood angrily watching her brother "training" his young horse. He was riding him in figures of eight, starting and stopping, to make him "handy for swordplay".

If he ever does swordplay on horseback he's more likely to cut the horse's ears off than be a threat to his opponent, Minna decided.

She was heartbroken to lose Silva. Since Cerdic had joined the army, he had claimed Silva and now kept him in the stables in the fort. This was men's territory where Minna only went now if the soldiers were all out on horseless duty, which wasn't very often. She wasn't a child any more. Cerdic had been quite happy for her to do all the work of raising and caring for Silva until he was ready to ride, then he claimed him. Minna thought this bitterly unfair.

"You promised," he reminded her.

The rashest, stupidest words she had ever spoken! But one did not go back on a promise. She knew that. And it was right for Silva to have a job. But Cerdic's lack of regard for her feelings needled her.

"I hate him!" she wept to her mother. "It is so unfair! He treats Silva like any old nag, and he isn't any old nag! He's a wonderful, fantastic horse, much too good for Cerdic. Cerdic doesn't deserve him."

If it were Theo, that would be a different kettle of fish. Theo had a devoted groom for his mare Pesrut. Theo would have liked to have had Silva, but was too honourable to claim him, although Cerdic was the rawest of raw recruits. Minna's mother thought that Theo was nervous of getting in Minna's black books if he claimed Silva and then did not treat him to Minna's satisfaction. Best to keep out of it. It was very easy to get in Minna's black books.

"Oh, you are so besotted with your horse! Grow up, Minna! It's only an animal. You should be thinking of your own home and marriage now. You're fourteen. It's a child you should be yearning for, not a horse. That young Esca has an eye for you and you give him no encouragement. He's a fine young man with good prospects. Your father wants you betrothed."

"I don't want it!" Only to Theo, she added to herself. Her mother knew that, of course.

"You look too high, my girl."

Without Silva, she had nothing. Only glimpses of Theo occasionally. She had never wavered in her love for him even when she scarcely saw him.

"You're just a silly child, wanting Theo. He will marry into the Roman world as soon as he gets promotion. Marriage is a way up to someone as ambitious as Theo. The tribune's daughter is a more likely match for him. Julia is very beautiful and Tiberius would like the match, I'm sure. I've heard it discussed."

"Gossip!"

"Yes, gossip." Her mother smiled. "It would be a boring life here without gossip."

But she was pleased her daughter gave the gossips nothing to talk about. With her proud scorn of smitten young men and her love for her horse, Minna was a strange child. Few boys dared to risk advances, although she was much admired for her looks. With her cloud of hay-gold hair, her fine skin and luminous sea-green eyes she was on the way to becoming a beauty. Tall and slender, she was quick and agile and brave and could swim like a fish. The boys found it hard to compete.

While Cerdic rode she had to hold onto his dog Fortis. Fortis was a year old, a beautiful grey-gold wolfhound bred by Cerdic from his bitch Mel. She had had six puppies and Cerdic had sold five of them to go to Gaul, for a lot of money. British hunting dogs were much prized abroad. The best of the litter, Fortis, he had kept. Fortis now never left Cerdic's heels, and had to be chained up when he rode out with the army. As Minna loved Silva, so Cerdic loved Fortis.

"You can have your stupid dog," Minna said, releasing him as Cerdic rode back to her. "Let me cool Silva off for you. You can't take him back to the stable in a sweat."

She knew he could, of course. He had no regard.

"Fine. You have him."

It was boring, cooling a horse off. Cerdic did not care for it. He slipped down from Silvas's back and turned to the excited Fortis, fawning at his feet.

"My lovely boy! Come for a run!"

"Go to Daddy, darling!" Minna mocked.

Cerdic laughed. At bottom, they understood each other. But they were going their different ways: Cerdic a hard, narrow-minded Roman soldier, Minna a wild, love-seeking young woman.

Cerdic gave Minna a leg-up onto Silva's sweaty back. At her touch on the reins he dropped his head and stood like a statue. Cerdic strode away with his dog, and Minna spoke softly to Silva.

"My lovely boy! You will always belong to me, whoever rides you. You know that, don't you?"

Almost as if in answer, Silva dropped his head meekly and pawed the ground with one foreleg. He always relaxed with Minna, after being stirred by Cerdic into a head-tossing, nervous accident-waiting-to-happen. The horsemaster of the troop did not think much of Cerdic's horsemanship. He had cited Minna as a paragon to copy, which of course annoyed Cerdic out of all proportion.

"What has a girl to do with horsemanship?"

The old horsemaster had not the words to find an answer. But he knew a horsemaster when he saw one, even if it was a female.

Minna rode Silva away out of the horse ground, past the workshops and drinking houses of the vicus, past the scattered living huts, shops and animal shelters until she was on the open road to the west, on her own. Then she turned his head towards the marshes that led across to the estuary, making for the firm sandy beach and the shallow waters of the river that ran inland from the sea. On the other side lay the whole of the east of England, ruled by the city of Camulodunum and its garrison, to which Theo was answerable. The river here was very wide, almost two miles at high water, with a strong tide running. It was easier to reach Camulodunum by water than it was by land, for the first crossing of the river was some fifteen miles upstream. Its shores were mostly muddy, but here at Othona there was a beach of fine sand and shells.

Minna rode there, savouring the peace away from the seething fort. She thought Silva liked it too. She guided him to the edge of the water and let him splash along in the shallows. Seawater was good for horses' feet. Theo often had the whole troop ride home on the edge of the river. Roman horses were practised at swimming for it could be necessary on expeditions across country, but none were finer swimmers than Silva. Minna had taught him early on, swimming alongside, holding onto his mane. But now he was strong enough to carry a man while he swam. In the summer when it was hot, Minna had often swum him for pleasure, but now, in October, the water was too cold for comfort.

"Not today," she said, as he turned to go deeper.

He obeyed her, tossing his long mane. Now full grown, he was as tall as most of the fort's mounts, just under fourteen hands, and his grey coat was still dark, the colour of a stormy sky. His mane and tail were black and his head refined, the eyes exceptionally fine and kind. Minna knew the old horsemaster swore by a horse's eyes. "They do not hide their hearts, as humans have learned to do." Cerdic said he was batty. But Minna recognized the light that shone for her in Silva's eyes. He would never transfer his heart to Cerdic, however long he was in his ownership. So she made the best of her brief times with Silva, even if it was usually only while doing the menial tasks that were too much bother for Cerdic. Cerdic preferred to spend his spare time with Fortis.

Minna rode slowly back to the road. An autumn mist was creeping in from the marsh, threading grey fingers across the waterways. Beyond, the forest lay dark and menacing in the depressing evening light. One could sniff danger on a day like this. Minna knew that Theo was jumpy, claiming that the threat from offshore marauders was not yet over, not until winter closed down sailing in the North Sea. There had been more of them this year, getting ever more confident as tales came of the breakdown of Roman authority in Europe after the death of the great Constantine. Now his son Constantius was emperor. For how long? He had already killed his brother, and now Minna had heard news of a revolt in Britain against the emperor by a Roman commander called Magnentius. If the Roman commanders themselves were leading a revolt against the emperor where was that going to land them all? Minna knew that Theo understood all these political ramifications, but to her it seemed like one long killing. Brother killed brother, sons killed a ruling father to take his place. Even a ruling father killed a son who grew too strong.

But the emperors were far away, and the only concern at Othona was to resist the predators that attacked them from the sea. These pirates came from poor and ravaged lands; they knew that England was a fair, fertile island full of wealth, of valuable tin and silver and cattle, with sweet land amenable to growing good crops, watered by fine rivers, its climate neither too hot nor too cold. Why should it belong to the Romans? Of course they came.

Othona had only one fast ship, not enough to attack when the pirates came in pairs or threes. The threat had not gone away and foreign ships appeared quite often on the horizon. If they came ominously inshore, Theo had to send smoke messages across the river to summon ships out of the Camulodunum river. He had asked for more sea power, but the command in Camulodunum said the pirates would never land because Othona was too well defended. They said they only preyed on other shipping. But Theo thought they would land if they stood a chance. This last week most of his cohort had been summoned away to help put down a disturbance on the Thamesis shore, and Theo had sent a force under Octavius, electing to stay himself where he thought there was more danger.

The fort now had only a skeleton crew.

Cerdic said, "I bet the ships out there know that. They've spies everywhere. They could well come while we're so few."

"Are you trying to frighten us?" his mother asked severely.

"No. I'm only saying what everyone knows. Why do you think Theo is staying, when you know how much he loves going inland for a fight?"

It was a good argument. Cerdic had been disappointed not to go with Octavius. Octavius had taken the seasoned fighters: Theo had given him his pick.

"Theo thinks there is more danger here. He has kept all the boat handlers."

"If the fog comes in, it won't help him," his mother observed. "It's the time of year for fog. He won't be able to send messages to Camulodunum."

Minna listened to this gloomy conversation which did nothing to lift her spirits. If the pirates managed to land, everyone would be in great danger. Looting, burning and killing always went hand-in-hand with invasion, she knew that. Also, she knew that young girls such as herself were in the most danger.

She would gallop away on Silva! No one would catch her then.

"If they come in to land, I shall take Silva out of the stable and gallop away on him," she said.

"He's an *army* horse! You can't just take him! Besides, the fort will be by far the safest place if they land. They'll never get inside it, you know that. Everyone will come inside, Theo will order them. It will be the only safe place. The gates will be shut and the pirates won't be able to get at us."

Minna considered. It was probably true. The enemy would raid the vicus and take what they wanted outside but they would never get into the fort. Even outside it, they would be within the fire of the bowmen from the ramparts.

"It's not going to happen! The gods forbid!" said their mother.

Their father merely drank more and did not get into the argument. He had made his own sword and spear and kept them by his side, Minna noticed. Cerdic lived in barracks now and was at the mercy of whatever Theo ordered. But there was great confidence in Theodosius Valerian Aquila amongst both the soldiers and the civilians. He had proved himself brave and strong for all his youth – and intelligent too.

It was strange in the fort with most of the troop missing. The ones left were on lookout on the ramparts or out on the quay. As the evening wore on, the mist thickened to heavy fog which fell in a white blanket to the very ground. One could hardly see two paces ahead. Beads of mist gathered on Minna's hair and eyebrows as she crept out into the street, looking for Theo. For once he would be alone. He might deign to notice her, or would he be too preoccupied with the danger? The oil lamps outside his house gave off a muted glow. She met him in the doorway, colliding.

"Minna!" He was wrapping himself in his cloak. "I'm going out to the quay," he spoke in a soft voice. "I want to listen. Go home and keep warm."

"I'll come with you!"

"Be silent then. I'll not argue."

He gave notice of his intentions to the guard on the ramparts and they went out by the postern gate in the north wall. If they hadn't the wall to follow, Minna didn't think they could have found the way at all. It reared high above them, dark in the fog, with just the hushed footfall of the guard on the top making an occasional creak on the wooden walkway. No one was speaking. The wet silence hugged them. The cold went through to the bone. Why ever had she come? Minna wondered. The answer sent a shiver through her, but not of cold. Close to Theo, his heavy cloak brushed her face as if with love.

They came round the north-eastern corner of the fort where the sea came up and the quay had been built below the wall. The tide was high and their ship the *Othona* lay afloat amongst the flotsam of the villagers' cockleshell fishing boats and coracles. Her heavy warps dipped and stretched as an uneasy breeze came from the north. Not a fair wind for pirates. But were they out there? Impossible to tell.

"We sit here and listen," Theo whispered.

Did he not trust the guards on the wall above them? Minna guessed not. Having given orders, he could now be sleeping peacefully in his house. But that was not his way.

He sat down on the quay, hanging his bare legs over the edge. The water lapped just above his feet in its lazy, ceaseless motion, black as pitch. Strange to think this was the same sweet sea she swam in, Minna thought, when the sun was high in the sky and the larks were singing. Now no birds sang, no stars shone; there was not a rustle in the grass and no reeds sighed. The world was dead.

"They are out there, I know it," Theo whispered.

The clammy fog wrapped them round. Theo shrugged one shoulder out of his cloak and pulled it round Minna so that their two bodies were close. But Minna knew it was only a kindness. His mind was in the darkness.

If they were out there they too were playing the same silent game. Minna thought Theo had it wrong, but the feel of him so close, his warmth warming her, took her mind off danger. She thought she could feel his heart beating. She could smell his lovely hot-baths smell, the oil Benoc rubbed him with – how pampered these tough soldiers were! And yet the hard edge of his sword scabbard rubbed her thigh and she knew his hand was more than ready to use the sword within. It was his father's sword, its hilt set with gold and precious stones. Like her ruby. Minna had never taken her ruby ring off, not since Theo had given it to her. He had never mentioned it since.

She sat quiet and still, listening. Theo did not speak. The night was black as pitch.

Then, away out across the water, a faint burring noise. Theo stiffened. It stopped, then came again.

"What is it?" Minna whispered.

"Anchor chain."

If the pirates were there, they were being silent too, creeping in to spring a surprise. But they couldn't muffle the sound of an anchor chain being laid.

"The tide is on the turn. They don't want to be carried away on the ebb," Theo whispered. "They are there, I'm sure."

His arm came briefly round her and gave her a squeeze, then he got up and took his cloak back round him.

"Come."

He took her hand and guided her back over the slippery quay to the wall, then they walked in single file back to the gate. The guard opened it and they passed into the torchlight.

"Tell the men to come down. I want to talk to them," Theo ordered. And then, to Minna, "Go home now, Minna. I will send word if you might be in danger. If they are going to attack, it won't be until the next high water, twelve hours away. So we have plenty of breathing space. If the fog clears in the morning we can send a smoke message to Camulodunum and all will be well."

So much for her hopes of sitting in his lovely warm house for a domestic evening! He had too much on his mind to bother with her and his anxiety now filled her with gloom. If the foreigners were to land and overcome the fort, the prospects for herself and her family were not good, she already knew that. She groped her way home and told her parents what was going on. But her mother was more annoyed with her for going to see Theo than bothered with the news she brought. Minna was fed up with being nagged and went to bed, shutting out all thoughts save that of being inside Theo's cloak, feeling his heartbeat. If only he had not been preoccupied with anchor chains!

VIII

She was awoken by a rough shaking. She opened her eyes and saw Cerdic's face above her, lit by a torch. He was shaking his head, a finger to his lips.

"Ssh! Don't wake anybody!"

"What is it?"

In the torchlight she saw that Cerdic was scared. He was appealing to her, no longer the cocky boy playing the big brother.

"I have to tell you – get dressed, Minna! Come outside! Hurry – I've no time! I need you."

Minna leaped to obey, wondering what on earth

was the matter. She remembered the threat from out at sea, the rasp of the anchor chain...but it was scarcely light yet. A dark dawn, the fog seeping into the house... She pulled her heavy woollen shawl round her and followed Cerdic outside. To her amazement Silva stood there, with Fortis lying at his feet.

"Oh Minna, listen – Theo has ordered me to take a message to Camulodunum to bring help – ships – to bring ships. He's ordered me to swim the river!"

"On Silva?"

"Yes, because he's the best swimmer of the horses. And me too. He says it can be done and I'm not to be afraid. But I am –"

Minna could see he was. He was suddenly only her stupid brother, not a Roman soldier at all.

"To swim! Why doesn't he send someone rowing?"

"Because the devils out there have been ashore and holed all the small boats. Theo's having the lookouts flogged – they fell asleep. He's in a great rage. I couldn't argue with him. He says Silva won't get lost in the fog – he'll know...animals know. I just hope he's right. I came to tell you, so that you know what's happening, to tell our parents. In case – you know...but I'm supposed to be on my way. I shouldn't have stopped off here. But I want you to take Fortis, else he'll follow me."

But Minna knew he wanted her.

"I'll come with you," she said sharply. "To the beach, at least, to see you off. Don't be afraid, not with Silva. Theo wouldn't have sent you if he thought there was danger in it. He must think highly of you, Cerdic."

She spoke severely, as if to scoff at his fear, but inside her she wasn't a bit surprised that he was frightened. So would she be! To swim across the river – nobody ever did that. Not that she knew of. Only far upstream perhaps, almost into the town where the ford was.

"We can both ride. I've got to hurry," Cerdic said. "Here, get up."

He legged her onto Silva's bare back and scrambled up behind her, and at a touch from Minna, Silva trotted off down the street towards the main gate. Fortis frolicked along beside them, excited by this unusual dawn run. The guard at the gate stopped them, but Cerdic called out clearly, "On the centurion's orders! Let me through!"

"Taking his girl to a safe berth, are you?" the guard jeered.

But the gate was opened. Did they really think she was Theo's girl? Minna wondered with a jolt of pleasant surprise. Cerdic was too disturbed to notice the allusion.

Minna said, "Once you're on your way it won't be bad, Cerdic. Cold and horrible but not really dangerous. Just hold tight to Silva. He will get you there, I'm sure."

She put Silva into a canter. His stride so smooth, it was easier than trotting. He stretched out, tossing his head, apparently able to see where the road was, which was more than Minna could. The fog was as thick as ever, even with the dawn coming. When she guessed the distance was far enough she pulled him up.

"I think the best place is where I usually go with him. You will land on firm ground on the other side, on the beach. If you go farther upriver it's all mud. You'll never get ashore through that."

"Yes, I know that," Cerdic said sharply.

"Here then, about here."

She turned Silva off the road onto the saltings and knew they were in the right place. Silva knew. Soon the shell beach was beneath his hooves. Minna could feel Cerdic trembling. Or was it the cold? The mist reached in through the warmest folds of her cloak with icy fingers. To plunge into the black river...no wonder Cerdic trembled. But he was a Roman soldier! Theo had picked him especially for this vital task. He should be proud. Silva pawed the water's edge as he always did, liking the feel of it. Minna knew she was as anxious for the horse as she was for Cerdic.

"Trust him, Cerdic. He will know where safety lies."

"I can't see a thing! How will I know I'm going in the right direction?"

Minna heard the squeak of panic in his voice as she slipped down from Silva's back.

"Keep athwart the tide. It's just started to come in, so you won't be swept out to sea. But you don't want to land in the mud upriver. It will try and take you, so you must steer with that in mind. But Silva will know."

Animal self-preservation would come into play. "Trust him, Cerdic," she repeated. "Go on now. I will look after Fortis, don't worry."

It seemed so strange, talking like a grandmother to buoy him up. She could hear herself sounding very old and wise. But in fact she *did* know the river and its ways as well as most of the boatman, because she played there and swam so much.

But it was a horrible moment, seeing her brother and her dear horse away into such danger. For, in spite of her reassurances, she knew it was a dire thing to be doing. Would Theo do it himself, she wondered, what he had so blithely ordered? But yes, she thought he would. No one doubted his courage. Cerdic's had never been tested. Now was his time.

"Don't be swept away from Silva, whatever you do."

Cerdic took up Silva's reins and urged him into the water. Silva thought to paddle, as usual, and turned along the edge but Cerdic turned him abruptly into deeper water. Minna saw the pony's hesitation, sensed his surprise, then there was a swirl of his dark tail and Cerdic's shout as the icy water breasted up over his seat on the warm horse.

Minna shuddered, almost feeling it herself.

"The gods be with you!"

Then, with a lurch of horror, she was just in time to lunge for Fortis and catch him by the collar. He wanted to follow Cerdic, and struggled and whined in her grasp. How strong he was! She nearly choked him, pulling him back from the water.

"Sit, you stupid dog! Stay!"

He was already wet and muddy, and churned and whined against her hand, getting her as bedraggled as himself. She wanted to stay and listen for Cerdic and Silva, but they must have got into deep water quite quickly, for after a few minutes all was silence out in the darkness. The fog lay like a thick curtain. Minna could tell that the night was over, that dawn had come, but it made little difference to the visibility. It was no more than five metres, both over the land and sea. From experience she knew that it could lie like this all day at this time of year, only thinning at midday, perhaps, if the sun came out. But their enemies were close enough to find them, she thought. In the stillness they would catch the sound of a lowing cow or barking dog to tell them where the land lay, even if the fort was ordered to silence.

She had to go back, although instinct told her to stay out here on the marshes.

What if the fort was stormed? Theo obviously expected it, if he had sent Cerdic for help. She had always thought she could flee on Silva if it happened, and take her mother too, but now there was no Silva.

"Come, Fortis. It's no good waiting here."

But the dog did not want to come. She had to undo a woollen tie from her hair to make a lead to take him with her. His beautiful golden eyes were full of distress and he whimpered softly as he padded along beside her. She could see how Cerdic loved this dog, so faithful and intelligent. It was a great favour to be so loved by a dog, and dogs did not hide their devotion. Horses were not so obvious.

"But I think Silva loves me as much as you love Cerdic, even if he doesn't make such a fuss about it."

As she looked for her way back to the road, she stumbled over a root. The leash slipped from her hand, Fortis whipped round and was away back towards the beach before she could snatch at his collar.

"Fortis!"

She dared not shout, and doubted whether he would come if she did. But she turned to go back, cursing, afraid the dog would go into the river after Cerdic. He wasn't afraid of the water, she knew, and always swam with Cerdic.

"Oh no, Fortis," she prayed, "say you haven't done that!"

What a fool she was, not to have had more care! She called his name as loudly as she dared, but no playful dog came bounding back to her. He was only a puppy after all, and often did not come back to his name, so she hoped to find him waiting for her on the shore. But when she got there there was no sign of him. There was only a line of deep, running paw marks going straight into the water.

Minna stared in dismay.

"Oh no! You stupid dog, you'll drown!"

Whatever would she say to Cerdic if the dog drowned? He would never forgive her. How would the dog find Cerdic, anyway? Did a man leave a scent on water? Minna had no idea. What a fool she was!

She didn't know what to do, only aware that she had failed Cerdic. She paced up and down the water's edge, staring into the fog. But there was no sign out there; all was silent. She started to cry, she couldn't help herself. She began to think they would all drown, not only the dog, but Cerdic and Silva too. She felt fastened to the spot, impossible to go back to the fort. As she stood the water crept up towards her and the deep paw-marks filled up with water.

"Oh, Fortis, you dear stupid dog!"

What devotion to put such trust in his master!

With daylight the visibility was clearing slightly. Even if it cleared she doubted whether she would be able to see Cerdic and Silva – they would be a mere speck on the water – but if she waited Fortis might realize his folly and come back. Just a chance – she must wait. Besides, she did not want to go home and have to explain what a disaster was in the making. Her mother would go mad with fright if she knew what Cerdic was up to.

But the fog persisted, lying thick on the water. Above, the sky was clearing, a hint of sun shining through. Did Theo want it to clear, or were they safer hidden? Minna could not decide. If the marauders wanted to land by the fort they could only do that at high water, which would be at noon. Minna doubted whether they would risk landing at low tide out on the mud and walking to the fort. It was far too dangerous if one didn't know the safe ways across. Cerdic had left when the tide was at its lowest. If he was successful, he might get to the garrison in time for them to put out to sea and reach Othona before noon. That was what Theo was banking on, she guessed. Whatever was going to happen? Minna felt herself trembling, and it wasn't only from the cold. They could all be dead by nightfall.

Suddenly she heard a sound across the water. Fortis, could it be?

"Fortis!"

If only he was coming back – that would be her greatest relief.

And then, out of the mist – Silva, breasting up out of the water with Cerdic clinging to his mane, and Fortis leaping ecstatically beside him, scrabbling onto dry land. They were all back, more than she had bargained for.

"Cerdic! Whatever...?"

He was sobbing.

"I can't – I couldn't – not when Fortis came – oh, Minna, whatever shall I do? And Silva kept wanting to turn back –"

He was almost incoherent.

"Cerdic, it's all right! Don't –" She went to him and wrapped her arms round him. Silva was at her elbow, nudging her with fluttering nostrils. The water streamed off him. He shook himself, like Fortis, who was sending clouds of spray in all directions. Cerdic was agonized by his failure.

"When I saw Fortis – I knew he would drown if I kept on. Why didn't you keep hold of him? I couldn't bear it, seeing him –"

"You came back because of Fortis?"

"Yes."

"How far across were you?"

"How could I tell? I don't know."

"And Silva was going strongly?"

"Yes, but he wanted to come back all the time. Because he knew you were here."

Minna wasn't so sure. Silva was an intelligent horse and wanted to live, after all. But she knew he would go in the right direction for her. She could see that Cerdic was making excuses. He was exhausted.

"I swam beside him, to save his strength."

That was usually how they swam the horses, swimming alongside, holding onto their manes.

"You should have stayed astride him! Even if I hold Fortis safely now, you'll never make it, the state you're in."

Minna saw failure staring them in the face. How could they face Theo, go back and mewl their failure? It was impossible. There was only one solution.

"Cerdic, I will go. Silva will go across for me."

"You! You're not a soldier! You can't!"

"It's only taking a message, not fighting, you idiot. I can swim as well as you, you know I can. Would you prefer to go again and me do nothing?"

"No, I can't!"

"Well, then. It's the only thing to do."

Cerdic was at the end of his tether she could see. He was in no fit state to go on: he would drown and drown her horse as well. She did not wait to argue. She took hold of Silva's reins and vaulted up onto his back. As she turned him into the water her whole being seemed to rise up in revolt – what was she doing?! Against all her instincts she pressed her legs strongly into his sides and the water came welling up her thighs like an icy grasping hand. She gasped at the shock of it – then sternly told herself that she had swum in icy water many times, what was the difference now? But the difference was that it had never mattered before, and this time there was at least two miles ahead of her, farther than she had ever swum in her life. And it mattered as life and death mattered, not only hers but the whole fort's.

Strangely, feeling the glorious strength of Silva beneath her, she knew that what she was doing now was much better than mithering about on the shore. After the first shock her mind flared into a sort of euphoria: what a challenge lay before her! Girls didn't do this sort of thing! She would rise to it, she knew, because Theo needed it. She was doing it for Theo. Doing it to save Cerdic's skin – if she was successful her brother's failure might be overlooked. To turn back from his duty to save his dog! It was wicked, yet she loved him for it. However was he going to explain it to Theo? He would be totally disgraced. The thoughts flitted through her brain as she settled to her long swim. Once Silva was swimming strongly the water lifted her weight and she swung her leg from over his back and lay alongside him, holding firmly to his mane. He pulled her along, and she kicked her legs for extra propulsion. He made no attempt to turn back now she was with him, and she just prayed they were going in the right direction. If they landed too far upriver they would find themselves in a maze of creeks where they would be hours away from the garrison. In the right place on the firm shore of Mersea island, they would be easily placed to deliver the vital message. She knew the far shore well enough, for she had been there often, fishing with

Cerdic and Stuf, but she had never been inland.

The fog low down on the water showed no sign of lifting. It was a sea mist, following the river. Occasionally Minna pulled Silva up to test how the tide was running, and each time it pushed against her right side, running strongly now. She headed out slightly against it. The water slapped at her face and she could feel her hair streaming out behind her. She swam with her legs and free arm to keep herself warm, more than because it was necessary. Silva's strength beside her filled her with confidence, although she knew that the distance was testing. He had already swum a good part of it, before she had started. She had no idea how far a horse could swim. A long way, she guessed, if its life was at stake. But Silva was still young, probably not at his full strength yet.

"But I trust you, Silva," she muttered. "Don't let us drown!"

He paddled steadily, holding his muzzle up out of the water. But he wasn't fast, his legs and hooves not having much propelling power. He wasn't a duck. Minna knew their progress, if steady, was slow. The sky was light now and she could hear skeins of geese flying over making their foreign cries – Theo told her they came in from frozen lands beyond even the far reach of Rome. How little she knew about the world! Even now, when she landed on the far shore, she didn't know the way inland. There was only one causeway off the island, she knew that, but how to get to Camulodunum she had no idea. How ignorant she was of her nearest surroundings! To think that Theo had come from Rome, and his soldiers were from lands whose names she had never heard of…

This was the most exciting thing she had ever done in her life. She would never forget it. If she survived! There was no sign yet of shallow water or any land ahead and she could feel that Silva was tiring. So was she. She stopped swimming and clung round Silva's neck, talking to him. He had always answered to her voice. Now, softly, with her head against his neck, she spoke encouraging words, words of endearment. She knew he would never give up, not until he could go no farther, but she wanted him to know it was no game. Horses only swam if they had to, and she had taught him to swim for pleasure, but this was more than pleasure. She could feel his strength gradually draining, and his breath starting to labour. She knew they were in danger of drowning, both of them.

Surely she could not do this to Silva! Not even for the fort... Cerdic had sacrificed the fort's safety for his dog, but now it was the other way round. Silva was giving his life for the fort.

"Oh Silva, keep going! We must be close!"

They seemed to have been swimming for hours. Thick mist still surrounded them. Minna could feel the cold probing into her bones; her teeth were chattering and she too could feel her strength failing. She had no idea how long or how far they had travelled and was grimly aware that the tide must be taking them now to where they didn't want to go. She knew it flowed far more strongly an hour or two into its cycle. Her optimism was fading and now she felt real fear. Drowning was a terrible death. She prayed to the gods of war who surely must be on her side.

"Please, please don't let us die! Not lovely Silva, please."

He did not deserve such a reward for his devotion. Not once had he tried to turn back, and still he struck out bravely, but she felt they were making little headway. If only she could see! They might not be swimming straight across by the quickest way, but at an oblique angle. There was no way of telling.

Silva let out a sudden snort and coughed. The water had gone into his throat. She felt him thresh out with a new, desperate energy, frightened, but he was sinking lower in the water.

"Silva! Try, please try!"

He mustn't give up! She too was drained of strength now, clinging desperately to his mane. She had it wound round her fingers. If he went under she would go under too. They would drown together.

Then she thought of Theo and the danger he was in. If the pirates landed he would be first into the fray and quite likely the first to be slaughtered.

"Silva! Silva!" she gasped. "We must – we must –"

The water hit her in the face and she went under. She hadn't the strength to fight any more and gulped in terror. She choked. She was drowning! Her body sank and her foot hit bottom. Silva was no longer beside her. Where was he? But, half-drowned, her feet were on the bottom. She cried out, laughed, choked and stumbled forward. Silva was standing, the water streaming off him. Minna staggered to him and flung her arms round his neck, sobbing with relief. They were on a beach with hard sand beneath them: the relief overwhelmed her. She fell down, still half in the water, and crawled agonizingly, clawing at the sucking shingle, until she found the beach dry and she was amongst the sea-wrack and the crab shells and the driftwood, thrown up like driftwood herself, completely exhausted. Silva stood shaking, head down, breathing painfully. Still the fog enfolded them, along with complete silence. No sound of life, no animal sounds, no dogs barking, nothing. Just the beach and, beyond, the marsh and saltings, exactly the same terrain she had started off from. Suppose they had swum in a circle! But no, from the way the tide was running she knew they had crossed the river. She threw a small piece of driftwood into the water and saw it start to bob slowly upstream on the current. She must follow the shore down to the right, seaward, and hope to find an army presence at the mouth of the river. She knew this stretch of shore, having fished there with Cerdic and his friends – sometimes with Theo – when they were children, taking their father's small boat. But perhaps she should ride inland towards Camulodunum? What instructions had Theo given Cerdic? She hadn't waited to ask. She cursed herself. Whatever way she went, it would take ages for help to get under way. It would have been quicker for Theo to have sent a rider inland to call Octavius back. But she guessed he wanted help from the sea in order to capture the pirate ships. Without reinforcements to help their ship *Othona* in the chase, the pirates would merely sail away out of reach, ready to threaten another day.

She didn't know what to do. But the fog decided it for her. If she struck inland however would she know what direction she was taking? She could wander in circles for hours unless she found the right road off the island, which she only would by incredible luck. If she followed the beach the way was firm and fast and there was no chance of getting lost. She knew there was always shipping going in and out of the river mouth because they could see it from the fort. There *must* be someone there who would help her!

Now the worst part of her journey was over she no longer felt relieved, but all the more anxious for what lay ahead. If only she knew what Theo's orders had been!

She went to Silva and laid her trembling hand on his neck. She was cold to the bone and beyond tears.

IX

Cerdic threw himself down on the ground and lay shivering with exhaustion and horror at what was happening. For Minna to go! To do the duty of a Roman soldier who had failed in his mission so ignominiously that he might as well kill himself! He now wished he had drowned, with Silva and Fortis too. When their bodies were washed up everyone would say how brave! Giving their lives for the fort!

He wept. Fortis crept on his belly beside him and licked his face, unaware of his part in the disaster. He thought it had been a jolly outing and now was puzzled by Cerdic's behaviour. He pushed his muzzle into Cerdic's face, whimpering.

"Oh Fortis, what shall I do?"

Why ever hadn't he stopped Minna from going? She was such a pushy, bossy girl – younger than him, which made her superiority far more galling. He had always resented it. It was one of the reasons he had been so keen to leave home and become a soldier, to put himself above her for a change. But being a soldier wasn't so wonderful. He hadn't thought it through and soon realized how much he missed his freedom. The hard work to maintain the fort and the eternal training drills were dreary, and the barracks at night in the company of so many older, foreign men were alien. He often wanted his mother!

And now he was in an impossible situation: to explain that his sister had gone on the mission when he had turned back... How could he do that? And if she succeeded where he had failed... How could he face the contempt that would arouse?

He hated Minna now – the arrogant way she had taken command, ordered him to stay while she went. He lay on the ground groaning with anger at her: at her arrogance, her confidence. He knew she would succeed. Where did that leave him? He would have to go away. There was no way he could face going back to the fort.

"You and me, Fortis. We'll go together."

But then he would be a deserter, an even worse criminal. He would have to get some clothes... dispense with his uniform. He was frozen with cold now, wet through, and could lie here shivering no longer. He would die. Maybe that would be for the best, for his body to be found on the shore...but then what would Fortis do? He groaned. By the gods, if only his mother were here...

Then he thought of the vicus, and their own hut outside the wall. All the villagers had been brought inside the fort for safety on Theo's orders, so there would be no one there to see him if he crept back. The hut would give him shelter and he knew there were old blankets in there and straw for a bed. No one would find him, not for a while at least.

He could hardly walk, he was so numb and stiff. Fortis pranced ahead, his long tail waving with pleasure. The fog still lay like a fallen cloud, thick and wet, over the marshes. But in the sky above it a misty sun was trying to come through. It was invisible, but gave a softness to the grey light. The gulls up there could be in the sunshine, without a care in the world. But Cerdic saw his world now as grim and heavy as the fog.

The village was strange, somnolent without the buzz of its workshops and the smell of cooking. Only a few hens pecked about. Most of the animals had been herded into the fort. It must be mayhem inside there now. Had Theo been overzealous in his precautions? Cerdic wondered. For there was no sign nor sound of an enemy offshore. It was true that the fort was now poorly defended, so many of the troop away with Octavius, but with the gates shut it was impregnable. But Theo wanted to capture the boats out at sea and that was the reason for sending the message for ship reinforcements. To do that would be a fine feather in his cap.

"I am depending on you, Cerdic. With that fine horse of yours and your prowess at swimming, I know you can do it. Better than any of the men in the fort."

But not better than Minna!

Cerdic swore at the memory. To be depended on – to fail. What worse ignominy was there?

He stumbled into the family hut and angrily tore off his dripping clothes. There was an old tunic of his father's in a chest and some blankets, as he remembered, so he huddled into these and lay down in the straw. If he hoped to sleep he was disappointed. Round and round in his head swirled the awfulness of his situation: not only his failure but the thought of being trounced by his sister, a *girl*. For in his heart he knew *she* would not fail, not with Silva beneath her. He could think of nothing else. He put his arms round Fortis and buried his face in the long golden hair of his coat. The dog wriggled with pleasure and his warm tongue came out again in comforting licks.

"I could never have let you drown," Cerdic whispered.

At least he had not failed in that. Only in everything else.

X

The shingly sand was firm and made easy going. Following the water's edge, Minna knew she couldn't get lost. But whether she would find anyone to help her this side of Camulodunum was in the lap of the gods. There were lookouts and troops at the mouth of the river Colne, she knew, but it was quite likely they were on the other side of the river where there was a village of sorts. She might have to make her way upriver, which would mean doubling back to find the causeway off the island, the only way off it. But even Cerdic would have had this problem. Theo's orders had been a throw in the dark. He must surely have had his doubts as to whether they could be carried out successfully. But worth a try, even at the possible expense of poor Cerdic's life. Not to mention Silva! Minna was aware of Theo's ambition. He was hard and brave and let little stand in his way. Perhaps not a man to love and be happy. But she couldn't help herself.

She was freezing cold and wet through but Silva's long-striding trot warmed her a little. With land under his feet Silva's exhaustion was thrown off and he seemed none the worse for his long swim. The fog was still thick over the water and visibility no better, although day was well advanced now. The tide was still running in and had a few hours still to go to high water. They had crossed when it was at its lowest, just starting to make. If the marauders were going to land at Othona, it would have to be at high water.

"Come on, Silva, the sooner we get the message through the better."

She nudged him with her bare heels and he broke into his gliding canter. It was easier to sit on his bare back at the canter than at the trot, and his warmth came up into her thighs and seat so that she stopped shivering at last. Her hair flopped in a wet mass on her back, the drops of water flying. If only the sun would come through! And she thought of poor Cerdic, abandoned on the shore with his faithful dog. However would he answer to Theo? He would be disgraced. And then she felt sorry for him and knew that she wasn't a kind sister. She hadn't given him much sympathy in the heat of the moment.

She tossed her head. No help to think of that now.

She met no one, not even along the shore – no beachcombers, driftwood gatherers, fisher boys. It was too thick and cold. Lucky Romans in their brick-built houses with the hypocaust roaring away outside, sending lovely warmth under the floor so that they could loll about in their togas inside as if it were a summer's day! What riches they had brought to the land with their civilized ways – not that much had rubbed off on the ordinary working Briton like her father. She had heard of rich ones who aped Roman ways and owned big villas, but she knew none. Their children were educated like Roman children by tutors, not – like herself – left to pick up knowledge however it came her way. She knew she was bright. Her Latin was far more fluent than Cerdic's, even than her father's, but she knew nothing of law and astronomy and figures, and could not even write. She longed to be more knowledgeable, but sewing tunics all day was stultifying. She wondered if she could get a job within Theo's household? If she succeeded in this mission praise would be heaped on her, and she might get a place as a reward! The thought buoyed her up, as nothing else was happening to lift her heart.

She thought she ought to have come far enough to see some signs of life. She knew at this end of the island the water was deep by a steeply shelving sandy shore and boats lay there quite often. Soldiers lit fires there and kept watch, coming and going.

Mostly going, it seemed.

She pulled Silva to a halt.

"Listen, Silva, can we hear anything?"

Silva stood like a statue, his long ears pricked up. The sea washed softly against the shore, a murmur; a gull squawked. Nothing.

"Walk on."

His hooves padded on the firm sand. He had to keep scrambling through inlets of water, or sometimes go round them and lose the shoreline. Soon they were heading north round the end of the island and Minna was beginning to despair. If there was no one here, she had miles of journey still to cover and it would be too late by the time she found anyone for it to matter. All that grief in vain! She pulled up. Silva put his nose down and scratched his leg. A gentle steam rose from his body.

"Listen!"

She was not mistaken. She heard a man laugh and the clink of a utensil. Quite close. The fog was thicker than ever.

"Is there someone there?" she called out. Her breath hung on the air.

"Here! Who goes?"

She turned Silva in the direction of the voice and after a few paces a man loomed out of the fog. He was a soldier! Minna almost sobbed with relief.

"Oh please! Please!"

She suddenly realized how spent she was. All the gristle seemed to go out of her so that she slumped over Silva's back, almost in tears.

"Hey, gel, what's this? Lost, are you?"

Another man came up, and Minna saw a brazier on the sandy shore with a group of soldiers round it. Her luck was astounding! How easily she could have missed them, how easily they might have rowed away before her approach! But she couldn't see a boat anywhere. There was a smell of cooking: a pot was steaming over the fire.

"I'm from Othona. I have a message from Theodosius Valerian Aquila."

"Are we supposed to believe that?" the soldier said, grinning.

"He sent the message with a soldier but the soldier drowned, and I brought it instead." Near enough the truth, and they needed hard facts.

"So what is this message?"

The other men had come up and stood staring at her. She could see no commander, just a group of bored, cold soldiers, fairly brainless by the look of them.

"Where is your captain?"

"Gone back to Camulodunum with Tiberius. We're waiting for the weather to clear."

Just her bad luck – there was no one in charge!

"There are pirate ships standing off Othona and our commander thinks they will land at high water. He wants help to capture their ships."

At least, that's what she thought Theo wanted. No one had told her what the message was, after all.

"We saw no ships."

"How can you, in this fog? They were there last night. We heard them."

I sat on the quay with Theo's arm round me, under his cloak, and we heard their anchor chain, she wanted to say. But didn't.

One of the men said, "They may be the ones that laid waste the settlement at Walton. Bloody murderers – that was three days ago. We know they're around."

"Yeah, well, it's nothing new. What can we do about it? We can't move without orders. We're waiting for the governor. He put back to the city because of the weather."

"You've no boat here?"

"No, the captain took it – we told you – to take Tiberius home for the night. He likes his home comforts does our Tiberius. And he's in no hurry to get to Londinium, as far as I know."

They were useless, Minna saw.

Most of them, she could tell from their expressions, didn't believe her story. "Since when did a commander send a girl with orders for the tribune?" one sneered.

"I told you!" she snapped.

She was wasting her time. If they had had a boat she would have wheedled a lift upriver; it would be quicker than riding. But it was wasting her time to stay any longer arguing. Her flare of spirits at meeting them hardened into grim determination.

"Thank you for nothing!" she shouted.

She pulled Silva round sharply to ride away but one of the men, silent till now, called after her.

"Wait a minute!"

She held Silva in. The man came up to her, an older man, and laid a hand on her rein.

"Are you riding on to Camulodunum?"

"I have to!"

"Go to Fingringhoe. That lies south of Camulodunum, on the river, and it's possible Tiberius is lying there. I know he was going to pull in there, to see someone, on his way back and if you're lucky you might catch him. And if not – and they believe your story – you can ask to be rowed the rest of the way. Tell them Armenius told them to row you."

One friend, amongst the dolts on the shore – Minna was grateful.

"Thank you! Thank you! I will do that."

"The gods go with you."

Perhaps, Minna thought, Armenius had a daughter somewhere: he was the only sympathetic one. She knew she would have a job to get her story believed. At least Cerdic would have been in uniform, a certified Roman soldier, while she must look like a five-year-old who had been caught by the tide when out with her shrimping net. But the man's sympathy warmed her and she rode on fast, encouraged after the initial disappointment. At least she was on the right road, and knew what was going on. She sang and shouted to Silva to raise her spirits.

"No one could have done what you did, Silva! You will have a laurel wreath round your ears and flowers beneath your feet!"

Silva, catching her mood, lengthened his stride on the sandy road. His long mane blew in her face. He thought she had gone demented. They came to the causeway which crossed the channel of water that made Mersea an island; the water was already lapping up to its raised, stony surface. Soon it would be under water, but they were in time to cross. She galloped, deluging two poor peasants who were lumbering across with faggots of firewood on their backs. They gaped at the beautiful grey horse and its manic rider, and called on their gods to protect them before bending to gather their scattered burdens.

Minna didn't care. She was on a mission and time was of the essence. She *must* catch Tiberius! She was desperate now, aware that, for all the success of her swim, still no one knew of the threat to Othona. Theo must have good reason to be afraid, to risk Cerdic's life. If the fort had been at full strength, she knew he would put out to accost the pirates, but this time there were two, at least, and possibly three ships out there, and only a handful of soldiers to guard the fort. The west gate, she knew, badly needed repair. A strong force with a battering ram and shields over their backs could break in if they tried hard enough. Once inside, if they overcame the soldiers by sheer force of numbers, all the inhabitants would be slaughtered. They spared no one, not even babies. She had heard many stories of their brutality. These terrifying thoughts sped through her mind as she pressed Silva on – what a tough pony he was! He galloped wherever the ground was firm enough and picked his way unerringly over the rough stones of the road.

But some two hours later, as she approached Fingringhoe on the bank of the Colne river and became aware of her likely welcome there – now covered in mud, although nearly dry – doubts flooded her. At least, if she could access Tiberius, he would recognize her. If…but she could not bank on it. And her thoughts turned to poor Cerdic, sobbing on the shore.

Whatever would he do? she wondered. He would be in the deepest disgrace. Even for friendship's sake Theodosius would not condone what Cerdic had done. Turned back for a dog! No doubt Cerdic would put the blame on Silva, but Minna would have none of that, not even to save her brother's skin.

If she were Cerdic, she would die of shame.

But she, too, was so far no more successful. The message had not been given. She drove Silva on, sliding and skidding down the muddy road to the river, where the Roman depot was sited. There were ships moored, she could see, but was Tiberius there?

XI

Cerdic felt Fortis stiffen to alertness. The long golden body that lay beside him warming his frozen limbs was awake and listening, ears cocked up. A faint, excited whimper came from his throat.

"Sshh!" Cerdic was instantly aware.

He propped himself up on one elbow. He could tell it was daylight now and as light as it was likely to get, for the fog had scarcely lifted. But there was movement outside and he could hear voices. He put his hand over Fortis's mouth.

"They're not friends, Fortis! Keep quiet."

There was laughter, and then shouting. The voices were foreign. Cerdic knew that the pirates had come ashore, come for the rich pickings in the abandoned vicus. Cerdic guessed that the wine-shop would be a big attraction, and the butcher's shop with its cooking grill still smouldering alongside, with big hunks of fresh meat left on the slab beside it. If they came searching, he was in real danger, likely to get a knife in his gizzard. Everyone save himself was safe inside the fort.

He lay considering. It must be about high water by now, he guessed – the water deep enough for them to have rowed ashore. He doubted they would bring their ships in, only the rowing tender, or tenders. They wouldn't have moored it on the fort quay, for from there they would have come under a hail of arrows from the ramparts above. They must have landed some way south of the fort, probably in the first inlet where the water snaked inland through the marsh. They knew there would be good stuff to steal from the vicus, fortuitously hidden in the fog. No arrows would find them, until the fog lifted. They would steal everything they could lay hands on, and then set all the huts on fire. That was how they operated. He was likely to be burned to death if he didn't get out. Maybe a good ending for him…

But even as he lay considering, a burst of rough shouting came from the doorway. The light was blocked out, and an enormous man stood there.

Cerdic was lying hard against the sloping inside wall, because that was where the straw had been pushed out of the way and he had been lying on it. He had rough sacks and blankets over him and in the dim light he thought the man would never see him. He clamped a hand over the hound's jaws and held him fast and shrugged the blankets over both of them as best he could while the man like a great snuffling boar turned over the few items lying about – a spinning-wheel, an old handcart, the ox yokes and harness – nothing of any use to him. He had a knife which he started to plunge into some hay bales for no obvious reason, possibly hoping to rout some rats – it was as if he had already visited the wine-shop, so stupid was his behaviour. Cerdic lay tense, ready to get up and run if the knife came near. It was all he could do to contain the eager hound, although Fortis was well trained enough to respond and lie still, but his whole body shook with excitement.

Luckily another man came to the hut and shouted, and the visitor turned to answer him. The man had a large amphora of wine in his hands, which was like a carrot to a donkey, for the stupid visitor gave a roar of delight and plunged away out of the hut to follow his friend.

Cerdic gave a great sigh of relief. But he guessed the hut would soon be fired.

"We've got to get out of here, Fortis," he whispered.

If they threw firebrands in the entrance he would stand no chance.

Where to go was another matter.

He found a piece of rope for a leash and, holding Fortis close, he crept to the entrance and looked out. He could see dim figures in the fog congregating round the butcher's shop. He guessed they were fairly desperate for fresh food. They had found a spitted oxen which had been cooked and abandoned when all the villagers had been ordered into the fort, and they were hacking off great lumps with their vicious, short-bladed swords. They were heavy, fair-headed men, nearly all in their prime as far as he could see, and with the demeanour of men who took what they wanted, without argument. As Theo knew only too well, a formidable enemy. Enough of them could storm the west gate, Cerdic thought, when there was only a handful of defenders behind it. Once they were full of good roast beef...! Cerdic felt a shiver of fear convulse him. He must get clear of the vicus without being in arrow-shot from the fort, for he knew the soldiers would shoot at anything that moved. He had already decided to make south towards the forest where, once clear, he would be hidden and could hole up in a charcoal burner's hut until he decided what to do. Whatever might happen to his parents and his soldier pals in the fort he preferred not to think about. He had enough on his mind to save his own skin.

"Come on, Fortis. No barking now."

He went quietly, walking tall as if he were one of their own. There seemed to be twenty or so, as far as he could tell, possibly the whole contingent. Going ashore must be a far better proposition than rolling at anchor in thick fog. No doubt the whole lot had come. They were all too busy sacking the food stores and the wine containers to take any notice of him, so he had no trouble sneaking out round the back of the shops away from the road.

It was only then, getting clear of the vicus and making south along the edge of the marsh, that it occurred to him that, if he could find their tender – wherever they had pulled it up – he could take it out to sea and leave them stranded. As long as they had left no watch on it.

What a possibility! He could be a hero!

His heart gave a great leap of hope. If only he could find it...and if it was still afloat...or, if not, was it too heavy for him to push into the water?

If! If! The doubts beat in his brain. Or was there a guard on it? Surely not, they were so confident, so big-headed...

If he could find it!

But Cerdic knew the marshes better than anyone in the fort – save perhaps Minna. He knew the most likely inlet they had found, the nearest to the fort, and he could tell by the ground beneath him where he was in relation to the water: here was the oxen watering trough and soon there was the dyke that kept the grazing animals in. A cow loomed up out of the fog, one which had gone missing in the round-up, and gave him a mild stare. Cerdic jumped the dyke and was up over the bank, Fortis pulling ahead.

Now soft shafts of sunlight came fingering over the marsh. Cerdic guessed the fog could clear at any minute. He knew its habit of rolling over the sea like a great blanket, rolling in as it had the day before, or rolling out just as unaccountably. It must be well past midday and past high water too. The weather often changed at the top of the tide. He could even feel the sun soft on his cold cheek, the start of a beautiful autumn afternoon, not a breath of wind, not a cloud.

If the fog cleared he would see the boat, but if the fog cleared he would be seen too, stealing it.

"Fortis, it must be here, in this outfall!"

He had come across the skein of water looping in from the sea where Minna swam and he laid fish traps. If the pirates had come before high water the boat would be lower down from where he stood. He started following its bank, hurrying, jumping over the deep muddy ditches that stood in his way, or ploughing through the wider ones. He strained his eyes to see into the murk ahead. A cloud of oystercatchers flew up in a bank of silver wings, startling him, and a big heron lumbered off, yellow legs trailing. Cerdic let Fortis off the leash to make progress easier and the hound ran ahead, leaping with far more elegance than his master.

It surely couldn't be far away! Or, in their eagerness, had they come long before the water could carry them in? He had no idea. Or was the boat in another inlet farther away? They didn't know the best way, after all; they were strangers to this shore.

But just as he was beginning to feel the awful deflating plunge of disappointment – at last, there was the boat, outlined in the mist. It was big, big enough to seat the crowd of men he had seen, its oars pulled roughly inboard, except for two which were stabbed upright in the mud to serve as bollards. Two heavy ropes tied the boat to them.

Cerdic flung the ropes off in a second. He saw that the boat was cumbersome and was likely to be a pig to manoeuvre out to sea single-handed, but there was no time to lose now that the fog was thinning and the tide was running out. The boat was still afloat but it very soon wouldn't be. Once the water went, then nothing would move this monster when it touched bottom. It was already touch and go. Cerdic flung himself on the bow and shoved with all his might. The keel scraped on the shell bed but at least the boat moved. Not easily, but grinding over the shingle. Cerdic knew only too well how fast the water left these gullies once the tide turned, and shoved frantically, now knee deep in the water with his shoulder to the bow.

The boat slipped away. Cerdic clung on, half pushing, half being dragged, as the boat slid through deep water then snagged on a shallow bit. Fortis leaped beside him, loving it. Cerdic was terrified he was going to be seen: already the open sea was becoming visible in front of him and the fog was no longer a blanket but lying in thinning streamers across the marsh. The sun was showing blearily as if rubbing its eyes from sleep. A glance back over his shoulder, and Cerdic was horrified to realize that now he could see the enemy still blundering about round the food shops – which meant they could see him if they turned round to look.

He prayed to all his gods, terrified. The boat was running now, but there wasn't room on either side yet to use the oars. The inlet was opening out, but slowly, and getting deeper. The water was up to his waist, ice-cold. He had to hang on, kicking and swearing. Fortis started to bark with excitement, thinking it was a great game.

"Shut up! Quiet!" Cerdic gasped.

Another glance behind showed him the first flare of flame in one of the thatched roofs. Simultaneously –

perhaps because of the hound's bark – a shout went up. He had been seen!

Now he must row – it was his only chance. The boat's stern faced the way it was going, not a great help, but there was no room to turn it round. If they came to a shallow patch, all would be lost, but he had to chance it. He clambered into the boat and called Fortis to join him. Shipping a pair of oars seemed to take for ever as his hands, numb with cold, fumbled the shanks into the thole pins. They looked so crock and ready to break – the whole boat was a wreck – he knew he would be lucky to get it out to sea. But he had no choice. No use running for safety now – he was cut off.

Now he was rowing – or attempting to, for the oars hit the bank as often as they dipped in water – he was facing his pursuers. He could see a hard core of men was after him, some half a dozen or so, apparently more determined than some of the others who were shouting out jeering hunting calls, probably too happy with food and drink to realize the danger they were in. His pursuers were coming fast, jumping over the gullies. One man in front, tall and lean, was far more athletic than the others. Cerdic, straining with all his might at the oars, watched him fearfully. The water was deepening with every stroke, but the boat going backwards was as clumsy as a cow and he dared not lose time by turning round. The boat was long and could easily catch on the bank if he fumbled it, then all would be lost.

He thought all was lost already, for the man was catching up with him. Fortis stood up in the bow and started barking at him, seeing him – leaping, splashing, staggering towards them – as if it were all a great game. He had found hard shingle bottom and although the water was up to his waist, he came plunging on, yelling like a maniac. Cerdic bent to his oars, possessed with fear. He could see that the man was also possessed with fear, one of the few drunken marauders who realized the danger of their situation. If their boat got away they were stranded. Desperation drove him.

By the gods, what an athlete he was!

Cerdic drove his oars into the now open water, terror lending him strength. The water deepening, the man started to swim, and he was no mean swimmer. Fortis was barking his head off.

"Kill him! Kill him!" Cerdic gasped.

If the man put a hand over the stern Fortis with luck would attack him – he knew the word kill. But by the way his tail was twirling with delight, the hound still thought it a game.

The man was only a few metres off. Cerdic was holding him, and the tide sluicing out was helping, growing stronger by the minute. But the swimmer had it with him as well. A few of his comrades were still with him but not nearly so close. The man made a despairing effort and Cerdic saw his clutching fingers make a grab for the stern.

"Kill, Fortis!" he screamed.

At the same time he wrenched an oar out of its pin, leaped to his feet and raised it to slam down on the man's head. Fortis lunged at the man at the same time as Cerdic's oar came down. The oar knocked the hound flying into the water but at the same time caught the man a glancing crack on the side of the head. Cerdic had a vision of a hideous face screwed up, yelling, then he lifted the oar and brought it down again, this time with better aim. The fingers opened immediately and slipped away and the man went under the water, his scream of rage, or pain, cut off abruptly as he went under. Cerdic knew he must take his one chance of turning the boat round so that her bows faced out to the sea, for she was scarcely a match for a strong swimmer, going backwards. And two of the other men had now taken to swimming in their desperation to catch him so, even if one was done for, the danger had not gone away. Fortis was swimming after him, but Cerdic could spare no hand to pull him aboard. He shouted to him in encouragement as he threw himself on the oars again, but cursed his ill-luck in knocking the dog overboard. Now half his fear was for Fortis.

Panic drove him. He was well versed in oarsmanship and turned the boat round with swift, sure strokes – but she was so clumsy! Getting her under way again was desperate. He hadn't struck his pursuer a killing blow, unluckily, for he was up and swimming again, and to Cerdic's horror Fortis was swimming beside him, coming after the boat. If only the hound had made back for land! The inlet had opened out now into the sea and a glance behind showed Cerdic two anchored ships out in deep water. The fog was receding in great swathes, the sun bursting through.

Oh, my dear gods, Cerdic swore, save me, save me!

He flung himself on the oars. The man was bound to have a knife! Yet if he caught up again Cerdic knew he could hold him off getting into the boat. Save that two other men were coming after him. He couldn't hold off three. And Fortis – oh ye gods, stupid idiotic Fortis was coming too, swimming alongside the pirate. He still thought it was all a game. Cerdic longed to stop for him, but instead he rowed faster and faster. He was winning. The man's stamina was running out and his strokes were failing. Cerdic's heart lifted as the space between them lengthened. He knew now he was safe.

But as he watched, the man gave up. He bawled out across the water furious oaths, screams of rage, as the whole parlous situation of himself and his friends filled his mind. They were stranded, cut off from their ships, their escape and, now the fog had lifted, in full view of the soldiers in the fort. And then, to Cerdic's horror, the man turned on Fortis, still swimming happily beside him, and gave him a great blow on the head. He attacked the hound as if he were Cerdic himself. His hands went round Fortis's throat.

Cerdic screamed at him. "No! No! Not Fortis! Fortis!"

All his instincts strove to stop him, to go back, but the other men were still coming and this time his pull of duty overcame his despair. He went on rowing. He flung himself on the oars with such an angry force that a bow wave came up under the stem of the hideous, clumsy boat and the tide lifted her on the swirling current that was pouring out of the saltings and carried her more and more swiftly out to sea. Through his tears of sweat and pain he had a blurred vision of the man and hound skirmishing in the water, the man still howling with rage, throwing the hound about like a rag doll with his hands round its neck.

Cerdic wept. Wept and rowed, choking on his tears.

XII

Even as she rode down the track to the huddle of huts that was Fingringhoe, Minna could see that there was no imperial barge lying there, not even a decent ship of any sort, only a few fishing boats and small rowing boats. Her disappointment brought tears to her eyes. All this blundering about the countryside and still she hadn't got her message through! The fog looked now as if it might clear soon; she guessed it was getting on for mid-morning, the tide still making. If Tiberius was to be any use to Theo he must leave when the tide turned, to go downriver on the ebb, for the tide was very strong in the river and to go against it would take hours. She had very little time now – he *had* to go within the next two or three hours, else all her efforts would be in vain.

She clattered down to the quay where the only signs of life were a knot of soldiers in an office there. Four of them were playing cards. Two were standing talking, and turned in surprise.

"This is army property. What are you doing here?" one of them said.

He was youngish, sharp-eyed. Minna could feel his glance needling her. She pulled herself up tall and scowled at him.

"I've come with a message from Othona for the tribune. From Theodosius Valerian Aquila. I was told Tiberius would be here."

"Well, you've missed him. He's gone back to Camulodunum."

"He's in Camulodunum now?"

"Yes, until the tide tomorrow."

"I have to see him, quickly."

She tried to keep her cool, biting her lip, but it was hard. She could see the disbelief, the scorn on the soldiers' faces. Then she remembered –

"Armenius told me to ask you to row me up the river."

"Armenius? You saw him?"

"Yes. I told him my story – I have been sent by the commander at Othona, because it is threatened by pirates offshore and he wants help. It's very urgent. Tiberius knows me – he will see me. But there's very little time. The fort at Othona is in great danger –"

She heard herself gabbling, desperate... These blockheads! They smiled, one even laughed.

Minna screamed at him: "Do you not see I'm not joking! I swam the river with my horse to get here, to get the message through! The pirates have holed all our boats! Are you just going to stand there and do nothing? Tiberius needs to go on this next ebb, that's what our commander asked. I have to see him!"

She was almost screaming. Her exhaustion was making her hysterical. It was perhaps the soldiers' fear of a hysterical girl on their hands rather than what she was saying that made them back down.

"All right! All right! What do you want us to do? We're on duty here. We can't leave our post."

"What, none of you?" Minna nodded her head towards the card players who were now listening to her tirade with interest. Her scorn was obvious.

"Give me a boat then and I'll row myself up there. I'll tell Tiberius how helpful you were. No doubt you'll be rewarded. Just look after my horse – he needs resting and feeding. Perhaps that's not too much to ask of you."

She slid off Silva's back, and had to grab his mane to stop herself falling to the ground in a heap. Her legs would scarcely bear her.

At this the two men looked slightly less cocksure, and one of them said to the other, "The boy can row her up there. He's not doing anything. Then we're rid of her."

"Yeah, good idea. "

A native boy was happily fishing off the quay and was called roughly to order. He was about fourteen, strong and lively.

"This girl needs to be delivered to the town. Take the fast rowing boat. That's orders."

The boy came forward, grinning, obviously pleased with his commission. The rowing boat was new, a little beauty. Minna looked at it and felt relief flood over her. There was still time, if the boy could row. She turned and put Silva's reins in one of the soldier's hands. This was the worst bit.

"My horse swam the river and came here like the wind. He deserves the best. Look after him well." Then, with an effort, she added, "Please!" And then, remembering, "He belongs to the army. To the Othona commander."

The soldier bowed sarcastically.

"Whatever you say, ma'am."

Minna wanted to kick him in the teeth but, with a wrench, turned away and slithered down into the little boat. The boy was already settled at the oars. She dared not look back at Silva. He whinnied after her as the little boat pulled away, and she had to fight back the tears that brimmed in her eyes. She mustn't give in yet, not after all she had achieved! But the job was not yet finished and until she had seen Tiberius all her efforts could well have been in vain. Suppose she could not get access to him? Everyone had eyed her with amused disdain so far, not surprisingly – only her temper and her quick wits had got her what she wanted. But the guards in the big city might be a harder problem. And time was running out... already the tide was nearly at its height. At least this made the journey easier, the boy taking short cuts over the shallow insides of the bends. He knew every inch of the way. Minna could not fault him. His long easy stroke sent the boat skimming up the river.

"What's all this then? Why the hurry?"

His accent was broad native, his breath quite unlaboured. Minna felt herself relaxing slightly, knowing there was little else she could do. She told him the story of her journey. He was impressed, and showed no signs of disbelieving her.

"I don't know Camulodunum," she said. "When we get there, can you tell me where to find Tiberius?" She could spend useless time searching, she knew.

"He'll be in his villa, most likely. That's at the top of the town. We can ask at the quay. His barge is there and they'll know what time he's due back."

Minna's heart leaped at the sudden thought that she might find him already on his barge, ready for the trip downriver again. What bliss if this was so! She strained her eyes to see through the now thin mist that persisted over the water: the soft, rolling fields and woods on either side were now clear. It was a perfect autumn day, the sky an almost colourless canopy with skeins of geese flying high towards the sea. If only all was as peaceful as it seemed! What sweet country this was compared with Othona, with little farms and homesteads dotted along the river and contented animals being herded by children... nothing like the bleak marshes and stunted forest of her home, with its dangerous bogs and wild boars – and pirates.

Camulodunum was the first city the Romans had settled, taking it by force from the native British tribes whose meeting-place it already was. The natives had resented it bitterly, and still did, if the stories one heard were true. It was famous in history for, in its prime, having been wiped out by the British queen Boudicca. Boudicca in her great rage against Roman arrogance and suppression had killed over thirty-thousand Romans before she was killed herself. Old days were full of bloody stories: things were much more civilized now. But true Britons were proud of Boudicca in their history – a woman too! In spite of her great burden of anxiety, Minna could not help feeling excited as they approached the city, for she had never in her life been farther than the shores around Othona, never even seen a town.

They passed a few fishing boats and transports of timber and stone being poled arduously round the bends, and then at last Minna could see buildings ahead and the masts of moored ships and the curve of the great city wall. It was enormous!

The boy went on rowing.

Amongst the merchant ships was an elegant barge, Tiberius's transport, waiting for his reappearance.

The boy shipped his oars, then back-paddled as the tide swirled them on. He hailed one of the men standing on the barge's deck.

"When are you due to sail? This tide?"

"No. Next." The man obliged.

Minna's heart sank.

"Bad luck," said the boy to Minna. "He'll be at home."

"Can you show me where it is?"

The boy hesitated. "I can take you. But it means leaving this boat. It's valuable."

"I will see that you are rewarded, if it's stolen. I promise."

The boy grinned.

But when they came to the quay, there was a fisherman he knew, who promised to keep an eye on it. He took their line and helped Minna up out of the boat, eyeing her curiously. The boy jumped up behind her. Crowds jostled round them and Minna saw an open gate in the sweeping wall uphill from the quay. Uphill all the way! She was so tired! Gritting her teeth, longing for Silva, Minna hurried after her boy saviour. He had caught her urgency and she could hardly keep up with him. No one challenged them at the gate, although there were guards and a guardhouse. The soldiers were playing cards, as usual. They stared at her, but made no move to stop her. Minna knew she must look like a beggar, with her half-dry, mud-spattered clothes, bare feet and bedraggled hair. But she lifted her chin.

There were plenty of people about, most of whom took no notice of them, all about their own business. Ahead were large imposing buildings like nothing Minna had ever seen before. The scale of them astounded her. She had heard of temples to the gods, but nothing had prepared her for the temple of Claudius, with its great stone steps up to the massive entrance pillars, the people in the square around it looking like ants by comparison. Their way lay straight ahead, where more imposing buildings crowded her weary sight. Is this the life that Theodosius was heir to, she wondered, with his high-born parentage and ambition? It put in perspective her own ambition of his requiting her love for him. She could never find herself at ease in such surroundings, so grand and inhuman. Certainly there were well-dressed, rich people in the streets with their slaves carrying their goods, but there were plenty of workers too who did not look a lot smarter than herself. Every colour of skin, many faces as golden-dark as that of Theodosius himself, surrounded her, along with the flat-faced pale Britons who jostled her as her guide turned right into a street that led past the amphitheatre. The amphitheatre! She had heard of gladiatorial contests and the dreadful butchery of prisoners and wild animals that took place in the Roman theatres, but had never suspected that it happened so near to home. She was less than a day's journey from Othona, yet it was another world here.

The boy took her to the gates of what he said was Tiberius's villa. There were two guards on the entrance. It was a very elegant place, set back from the road amongst trees, a house with a courtyard round it, shutting out the noise of the street. Minna and the boy stood, irresolute. The boy gave Minna a nudge.

"Go on."

Minna stepped forward.

"I have come with a message for the tribune, from Theodoius Valerian Aquila, commander of Othona."

They laughed.

"You must be joking, darling!"

Minna's temper blazed. After all her trials and dangers, to be laughed at by two yobs who did nothing but stand around a gateway all day was too much for her.

"I demand to see the tribune! If you ignore this message you will pay dearly for it! I swear to it – you will be punished."

Her eyes blazed and her white cheeks flushed with anger. They exchanged glances.

"She's a strange one, this." They looked awkward now. "Since when did commanders send messages by a girl?" one of them sneered.

Before Minna could answer someone came up to the gate behind her, a woman with two slaves in tow. The two soldiers stood back obsequiously. Minna looked up and recognized Julia, Tiberius's daughter. She had seen her at Othona once or twice. She was the one her mother said it was likely Theo would marry, a match to be made for political reasons. However, seeing her at close quarters, Minna did not think

Theo would jib at politics this time. She was extremely beautiful.

Now was Minna's chance.

"Your guard won't let me in, ma'am, but I have brought an urgent message from Othona."

"From Theodosius?"

"Yes, ma'am, for your father."

"You look famished! Aren't you – I've seen you at Othona – you and your brother were playmates of Theo when you were children? He is fond of you, I think. His little spitfire he calls you – Minna, is it?"

"Yes!"

Minna's weary heart lifted at last. Theo had spoken of her to this high-born lady! To hear those words was worth all her pain.

"Come then. Message or no message, you look as if you could do with some food and drink and a hot bath."

She swept on and Minna followed, weak with relief and gratitude. At last! Just in time, she remembered the helpful boy, and looked back. He was out in the street, still grinning, and raised an arm in salute. She waved to him – a real friend in need – how lucky she had been at last.

The soldiers and the slaves glared at her, giving her passage, and she smiled at them and followed Julia up a drive planted with splendid clipped trees and into the courtyard. It was so elegant and beautiful; Minna had never seen anything like it. A fountain played in the centre and flowers grew in big earthenware pots against the walls. Long windows opened all round from the single-storeyed brick-built house. On the orange tiled roofs doves fluttered and cooed as if in Rome itself, and cats and hounds lay in the sunshine.

"Oh, how lovely!" Minna could not help herself.

Julia turned to her and smiled. "Othona is a bleak place! I wouldn't like to live there."

Minna thought if Julia married Theo, Othona would be her home. But then, with Julia's influence, Theo would no doubt be promoted to a more civilized post. Minna was so weary that silly thoughts flitted through her mind. Nothing much mattered now but to deliver her message and sleep.

Julia led her into the house.

"Shall I call my father and you can tell him your news? And then you can eat and rest?"

Tiberius came and Minna told him what had

happened, the truth this time, including Cerdic's failure. She did not see how covering it up would help now. She told him she had met his soldiers at the mouth of the river and at Fingringhoe, but they were all awaiting orders from himself before they would move. She could see that he took her story seriously.

"If those are the marauders I think they are, to capture them would give me the greatest satisfaction! They are an evil crew; they stop at nothing. They wiped out a whole village just up the coast, including all the women and children."

He rapped out some orders to the servants and they all went running.

"I will go at once. I will start my journey now, on this tide. The weather has cleared and no doubt Theodosius has sent signals across the river. When I get down there I'll know what's going on."

He was a middle-aged man, perhaps bored with the life in this now cultivated and peaceful city. The days of Boudicca were long gone. Minna had heard that his wife yearned to return to Rome, just as Theo's mother had. Minna found it hard to picture a city bigger and busier than Camulodunum – what a bumpkin she was! But Tiberius was kind, calling her intelligent and brave.

"You've done well, child, bringing this news. I shall commend you to Theodosius."

News of battle seemed to have given him a new lease of life, for he got everyone scurrying to see him on his way, shouting out orders, ordering horses to take him down to his boat. He kissed Julia hastily.

"Tell your mother what's happened. I can't wait to say goodbye."

Julia saw him to the door, then came back laughing. "Peace at last! We've the house to ourselves, how lovely. Come, let's get you clean and rested. And you must need a drink…"

She got her own servants scurrying just as her father had. A slave brought Minna the most delicious honeyed wine and some newly baked cakes and then there was a bath in the house's own bathhouse, with slaves to wait on her and wash and comb her matted hair and massage her with expensive oils and perfumes such as she had only ever smelled on other people – it was like being in another world entirely. Julia gave her one of her own beautiful embroidered tunics to wear, and a gauzy silken scarf to drape over her shoulders, and sat with her while the servants plied her with a plate of fish in a wonderful sauce and cheese on wheatmeal biscuits and fruit soaked in honey and wine. She was so hungry! But she tried to eat in a mannerly fashion, as she had sometimes tried to practise at home, to be fit to eat at Theodosius's table: now, with Julia hovering over her, she did not want to expose herself as the peasant she undoubtedly was.

But Julia was not a bit superior. She was only about seventeen, thin and active, with rather wild red hair and a strident laugh. She obviously enjoyed life – and why not, Minna thought enviously, in this beautiful place? Julia wanted to know all about Minna's journey, and her admiration was not feigned. She said frankly she did not want to go back to Rome – she scarcely remembered it – and hoped she would marry a man who had no Roman links. Minna wondered if this man was Theo, but she was now so tired that it didn't matter to her any more. She could not get her head round anything any longer. Julia quickly noticed and led her to her own room where there was a couch and blankets.

"Here, you must rest. We'll have time to talk later."

"My pony – Silva –"

But Minna fell asleep almost while she spoke. Silva was safe for now but her last thoughts were about getting back to him. She could not bear to think that he might be feeling abandoned, deserted by his friends.

XIII

In the morning Julia rode with Minna back to
Fingringhoe. She lent Minna a pony from Tiberius's
stable and they rode with two guards behind. Minna
had thought she would have to walk, so found herself
enjoying being treated as a lady when the crowd at the
gate gave way to their guards' imperious cry. I could
get used to this, she thought, smiling. Julia had found
her a tunic of very fine wool in a lovely blue-green
weave which she said she didn't want any more, and
a heavy cloak in matching turquoise; her old clothes,
freshly washed, were bundled up in a saddlebag,

along with copious honey cakes, legs of chicken and flasks of sweet wine to eat on her journey. No more swimming! She was riding home up the river to the proper crossing ford, and back down again along the shore, a day's journey at least.

"I shall have to leave you at Fingringhoe," Julia said, "but my guards can travel with you, to see you safe."

"I would rather ride alone," Minna said.

Julia was doubtful.

"My father would wish you to be accompanied."

"Silva is so fast, I am safe enough," Minna said. "I'm used to looking after myself."

Julia laughed. "Yes, I'm not so tough as you. My father guards me like a rare plant. I hardly ever ride alone."

Minna was desperately anxious to see Silva again. She did not trust the sceptical soldiers she had left him with. But when they got to the depot she was relieved to see he was in a comfortable shed with food and water. He started round at her voice and gave her his deep welcoming knucker of affection. Minna ran to him and hugged him, one of her greatest fears dispersed. Although he had been fed and watered, no one had groomed him: his coat was curled with dried sweat and he was still covered in mud. She had wanted to impress Julia, but had to be content with Julia's wise comment, "How well made he is! He's all quality. He's a hero, making that swim safely. Theodosius will have to reward him, make him a Roman citizen! See how he loves you!"

Silva was nuzzling Minna affectionately, ears pricked up. He had thought himself abandoned, Minna knew. He had never been away from Othona before and did not care for his strange surroundings. She kissed him on the muzzle and pulled his ears gently. She wanted to be on her way back now, alone. Everything was now in order, her mission safely accomplished, but she had no idea how the fort at Othona was faring. Theo had believed the danger very real, and whether the fort had been attacked or not she still did not know. Her own fears were still with her. And Julia was now her friend: they embraced affectionately, having enjoyed each other's company.

"I hope all goes well at Othona, perhaps I will see you again soon. My father said something about meeting him there when he comes back from Londinium. He knows I like trips out. If I come, I will make sure I see you."

"I would like that," Minna lied, thinking of how Julia would find her sewing tunics in her mother's untidy workshop. Perhaps Theo would send for her if Julia came, and wine and dine her as Julia had done, to reward her for her success in getting help? She lived in hopes! But she knew she was not in that class.

"Thank you for your kindness. And your gifts."

She rode back up the track to the main road to Camulodunum where they went their separate ways, Minna alone and Julia with her two guards. Julia had drawn her a map of the way with a stick in the sandy path, how to cut straight across country to the river crossing, and it seemed plain enough, well trodden through fields and forests. The fog had cleared early with the appearance of the sun, and it was now a soft, still autumn day without a cloud in the sky.

At last, cleared of her immediate anxieties, rested and well fed, Minna tried to enjoy her ride, her darling Silva beneath her, kind and willing as ever. She had never had such a fine ride ahead of her, her times these days with Silva snatched, with scarcely any riding. She went fast, loving the feel of the pony's smooth canter and his eagerness, not needing any heel or encouragement. The sun shone with autumnal sweetness, warm on her face, and the birds sang all round her, the geese creaking overhead in their long skeins of flight and the gulls falling around the sky like blown pieces of cloth. The road was good, well made by soldiers, no doubt, and the few people she passed waved to her with goodwill.

But all the time she could not put away her fears for what might have happened at Othona. Theo had not been so worried for nothing. She too had felt the ominous threat from across the silent, fog-bound water, and knew something of the brutality of the people they were up against. The thoughts were not encouraging, and she tried to put them down, telling herself that the fort was invincible.

She crossed the river at last by a wooden bridge at the foot of a steep hill up into a large village. There was a small army camp commanding the river, but no one apprehended her. The soldiers only stared and whistled. She thought they took her for someone high born, on her beautiful pony, dressed in Julia's lovely clothes, for she noticed respect rather than scorn in their faces. She lifted her chin and thought of the luxurious life she had just tasted, and wondered if she could ever aspire to such riches. Yet she had never been unhappy at home; until now she had never known what she was missing. Would she change anything? With her dear pony under her and the thought of Theo shortly to be commending her for her success in taking his message, she could not complain.

Silva's eager stride bore her away, facing home now along the south bank of the Blackwater river. They had to skirt inland around the many inlets and creeks but Silva knew he was heading for home and the miles did not tire him. His stride lengthened over the grassy track, not yet mired in winter rains, and the sun started to slip out of its zenith behind her. She would be home before dark.

But the nearer she got to home the more she began to wonder what had happened while she had been away. Cerdic's disgrace was so dire she did not want to dwell on it, but she was suddenly afraid that – after all her efforts – perhaps the marauders had attacked the fort and then – who knew what might have happened? The fort was fatally under strength. Her parents, her friends, even Theo, might all have been slaughtered! She remembered the evil faces of the ones Theo had captured earlier. They were a formidable enemy. And in the fog, their chance of landing had been good: Theo had had the sense to appreciate that. A cold fear now overtook her spirits. She was feeling very tired now, not used to riding so far, and her head ached, sick with foreboding.

As she came nearer to Othona, recognizing the ground, she dropped back into a walk. Her mind went again to her brother and the disgrace he must have suffered. She wondered how he could have dared walk back into the fort with such a miserable story to tell. He might be now in the soldier's jail, or have been flogged for dereliction of duty. The awful thing for him would be learning that his sister had succeeded where he had failed. Tiberius would have told of her arrival in Camulodunum – that is, if he had made a successful passage and been able to chase off the marauders and land at Othona. There was no way of knowing what had happened in her absence.

The fort was quiet as she approached. Out at sea there was no sign of any anchored ships, although the fort hid from her view any ships that might be laid at the quay. The smell of cooking came from the vicus as usual at this time, but mixed with it was the smell of burned straw. She could see some of the huts had been burned and were still smouldering, so knew there had been trouble. But there were plenty of people about, apparently unconcerned. This was no scene of slaughter and mayhem, only of a slight skirmish.

"Thanks be to Mithras!"

She felt a great weight lift from her spirits. The guards on the ramparts saw her approach, and to her amazement the trumpeter was called. A victorious fanfare rang out over the fort. The village people were shouting greetings and running to meet her. Tiberius must be safely here, to have spread her story! How wonderful that she was dressed in Julia's beautiful clothes – if only she had stopped to groom Silva properly!

After the first shock a delicious pride overtook her doubt and she lifted her chin and laughed as she went in through the gateway. Up the road between the swarming buildings, and now she saw Theo himself coming to meet her and at his side her brother Cerdic, showing no signs of disgrace at all… Her head whirled in confusion. As the slaves came to take Silva's bridle, she slid down off his back and nearly fell, so stiff with so much riding.

Theo came up and embraced her and she buried her face in his best toga, almost sobbing now with relief. She had not expected such a wonderful welcome, more aware of all the things that had gone wrong rather than the things that had gone right. It was wonderful to have Theo's arms round her, even if the embrace was one of congratulation, not love. Or was it? When she lifted her tremulous face she saw his lustrous dark, dark eyes looking down on her with what could only be love, his lips murmuring endearments: "I was so worried for you, my little Minna – so brave! So sweet! Thanks be to the gods to have seen you safely home!"

For those few seconds he forgot his status. But Tiberius was beside him with all the high-ups in his retinue, and almost as soon as the words left Theo's lips his arms put her away from him, and he became the commander again.

"You have done a great service to the state, and your brother too. You will be richly rewarded. Come and eat with us, and you will tell us your story and we will tell you ours. Thanks to your brother, we were able to round up those pirates. Now they're all chained in our prison and their ships are ours along with all their booty. It is a great day for Othona."

He sounded very pompous and commanderish in front of the tribune and Minna almost giggled. When

there was no one around he was just the same boy –
the Theo she had played with and grown up with, but
when he was being the commander he was a different
person. The responsibility was changing him. Perhaps
in a few years he would be a boring Roman tribune
like Tiberius. Yet he had never shown any inclination
for the easy life ruling in a defensive position from a
city. He had stayed several times with Tiberius but
had never spoken enviously of the life Minna had just
sampled. Strange, Minna thought, to prefer hardship
and danger. But that was what she admired in him: his
hard athleticism, his dreams, his imagination, his
courage. He wasn't just a pretty face even if, now, he
looked as handsome as she had ever seen him,
primped and perfumed for his hosting of the tribune,
his black curly hair closely cut to the smooth, freshly
shaven dark-gold skin, his best toga and tunic so
elegant (thanks to Minna's mother) draped around the
lithe, slender figure: Minna had rarely seen him look
so impressive. She just prayed that Tiberius was not
seeing what a suitable match he would make for Julia.
For him to be lured to the luxuries of Camulodunum
and she left mouldering in this swarming backwater
of a fort without him…it would be too much to bear.

She was taken into Theodosius's house where a meal was being laid out in the triclinium. She had timed it well.

"If you are not too tired, you will dine with us?" Theo invited her. Just as she had dreamed!

When the tribune and his retinue were to be entertained, Theo could offer hospitality almost as fine as Minna had experienced in Camulodunum. Minna had never seen the slaves so busy – with, she noticed, quite a few soldiers helping out and a slight atmosphere of panic in the kitchen. She sat on a couch at the table and hoped she would keep awake over what was likely to be a long-drawn-out meal. It was going dusk and Benoc was lighting the torches: the golden firelight fell seductively over the lavishly spread table and sent scurrying shadows over the walls as the dishes were brought in from the kitchen. Minna noticed she was the only female there. She had done a man's job, after all. Cerdic was next to her.

"So why are you a hero, after what happened? I expected to find you in prison."

Cerdic told her his story. "But they killed Fortis," he told her, choking back tears. "I have to go and find his body, Minna, after this meal. I must give him a proper burial. He is a hero as much as anyone. I won't rest till I find him. The moon is full and he could well be washed up on this high tide and left where the driftwood collects."

"Oh Cerdic! I will come, I will help you." Minna knew how he loved his dog. She knew how he felt – as she would feel if it were Silva. She tried to change the subject.

"So what happened, after you rowed the boat out?"

"Well, they were stranded ashore. The fog cleared, so Theo ordered the army out – what there was of it – and they rounded them all up. Well, most of them – some got away, I suppose. I could see their two ships were unattended – they had all come ashore, so I rowed back to the fort and got a hero's welcome. At the same time we saw two Roman ships coming across the river and knew that your message had got through. They went aboard the pirate ships and brought them back to our quay – that's where they are now. They are full of loot – they were on their way home to Germania; this was their last throw before sailing back – stupid greedy idiots to try here! They knew the fort was denuded, apparently. They seemed to think they could take it. They are mad. Theo has been grilling them in no uncertain manner, right up to when Tiberius arrived. Tiberius is going to take them back with him and they will be killed."

Minna then told him how her journey had gone.

"Silva will do anything for you," Cerdic remarked. "He's not the same with me."

"He would have taken you if you'd demanded it."

"Yes, it was my fault we turned back. For Fortis." He sniffed again. "I want to go looking. The tide is making now and perhaps it will bring him back. I must find him."

"We can leave shortly. I'll say how tired I am. They are talking politics, they don't want us now."

The men were drinking and, after a polite interval of time, the two of them slipped away from the table. As they intended, their departure was scarcely noticed. Save by Theo, whose eyes followed Minna's slender figure as she left the hall.

XIV

The fort resounded with the soldiers' drinking and carousing over what counted as an army victory. There had been no such excitement for several months, not since the last pirate attack – anything was an excuse for celebration in this backwater of the Roman Empire. Minna and Cerdic scurried along with their heads down, not wanting to be recognized.

"I can't go out on the saltings in these clothes," Minna said. "I must change. I shall never have such a lovely cloak as this again."

"Well, be quick about it."

"Mother will want to talk – she's bound to! I'll be as quick as I can."

Their father was out drinking, as usual. The workshop was still warm from the forge fire. They passed through into the back room where their mother was talking with some neighbours and drinking honeyed wine.

"Minna!" She sprang up.

But she knew what had happened. How the story had spread! The women clamoured round Minna, full of congratulations, and exclaimed over her beautiful clothes. Cerdic stood glowering in the doorway, willing her to hurry. She explained what they were going to do, and her mother understood, although she prattled on about how tired she must be and ought to be in bed.

"You know it matters, mother, to lay him to rest properly, poor hound. Cerdic will not grieve so. We need to be there before the tide turns."

"Well, be careful. Don't stray from Cerdic – the men have been drinking heavily tonight. It's not right for a girl to be out so late."

"They won't see us, mother."

The usual mother's remonstrations – did she not

realize that Minna was no longer a girl, but a young woman, a friend of the tribune's daughter? Minna quickly put on her old clothes and went out determinedly to join the fretting Cerdic. They left the fort and took the old familiar path round the wall and out to the seashore.

At the quay lay more ships than Minna had ever seen: their own *Othona*, the two pirate ships, and several Roman ships including the tribune's barge. A couple were anchored off in deep water; the others lay still grounded, their masts tilted against the gauzy stars. There was no breath of wind, no fog, no clouds, just a sky almost white with stars and a moon like a great silver platter gashing the sea with its reflection. They could hear the tiny waves breaking on the mud, like whispering; softly, softly as the tide came in, pushing its cold fingers into all the clefts and gullies, sliding like silk over the gravel. Cerdic started to cry again, for all that he was a Roman soldier.

"It won't be so bad if I have his body," he excused himself.

"He could be farther down, or even up the river. But never mind, we'll look as long as we can." Until I fall asleep standing up, she added to herself. But at least the banquet had put new strength into her. She felt the familiar icy mud squeezing up between her bare toes as they made their way out to the edge of the water.

"It will be best if we go two ways, you to the north and me to the south."

"If you find anything, shout me."

"Yes, and the same for you."

How far must she go? Minna wondered, as they parted. It was icy cold and quiet as the grave, save, faintly from the fort, the sound of drunken singing. The moon, riding high, glared down to the horizons, not kind like the sun but probing bright, hiding nothing. Cold and cruel, but the best light for what they wanted. Nothing moved out there, not even a wading bird. Even if the dog's body lay there, it could well be hidden in a dip or channel. There was no way she could search every indentation. But her eyes were sharp and she walked on along the edge of the tide, hopeful, finding rest from her own adventures in the calmness of the night and the beauty of the moon-slashed sea. There was no call from Cerdic. Poor Cerdic. Her heart bled for him.

She walked a long way from the fort, heading

south, following the encroaching water. Sometimes she was in deep soft mud, sometimes on cockleshell or on hard sand. Her eyes turned inland, searching the tumbled sea lavender and the green samphire. Twice she saw humps and went to investigate, but found only driftwood, the detritus of wrecked ships. She had seen bodies brought in from these marshes, of drowned sailors, not mere dogs. The waters were treacherous and sailors who did not know them foundered more often than not, grounded on hard sand far offshore, their ship pounded by waves until the bottoms gave way. Minna did not trust the sea, but loved it hopelessly. She would not like to live inland.

But it was cruel and cold tonight, advancing in a slippery, silken froth between her toes. It wasn't possible, even in this hard light, to find a dog's body in this tangle of marsh grass. She turned back, so tired suddenly that she thought she might fall. And as she did so, she heard a sound that made her heart lurch – a faint whimper.

"Fortis?"

It came again, slightly inland, back from where she stood. She crept into the thick sea lavender, calling the dog's name, and saw something move, as if waving to her. The dog's tail? She stumbled towards it, calling his name.

"Oh Fortis!"

The dog was lying on his side, too weak to move, save feebly wag his long plumed tail. Minna fell down beside him and cradled his head in her hands, putting her face close, sobbing with relief. Fortis licked her hands and whimpered. His tongue was warm, but his body shivered, the beautiful golden coat plastered slick to his bones with mud and detritus. He was near to death, Minna thought.

She stood up, cupped her hands round her mouth and yelled with all her might.

"Cerdic! Cerdic!"

If he didn't hear her, she would never move the dog on her own, and if she left him she would never find him again. The advancing tide was now quite close.

She screamed again and in the still night her voice seemed to echo from the horizon.

"Cerdic!"

Surely in the night silence her voice would carry to him? And yes, in a moment, from far away, she heard an answering shout. He would run now, she knew, splashing and gasping along the waterline. She kept yelling to guide him, and lay beside Fortis cuddling him, trying to give him her life's warmth. His feeble tongue flicked at her hand. And as she lay waiting she thought of the time three years ago when they rescued Silva from the same marshes. He too had been on the point of death. If only Fortis could be as lucky, his will as strong! When Cerdic came, that would give him the courage to survive.

"Minna?"

"Over here! He's alive, Cerdic! He's alive!"

Cerdic stumbled towards them and flung himself down beside his beloved dog. Fortis's tail lifted feebly.

"Oh be careful, Cerdic. He is so weak. He might still die."

"No! He won't! He won't. We'll carry him home. The tide is nearly here. We must hurry." Cerdic was almost sobbing again, but with joy and amazement.

But the big dog was so heavy. The two of them stood hesitating, considering, not sure how to lift him between them, then Minna said, "If we lay him on my cloak, perhaps, and sling him between us?"

She had pulled a rough bit of blanket round her shoulders when she left – calling it a cloak was to flatter it, but it was good for the job. She thought fleetingly how lucky she had changed, else it would have been Julia's beautiful garment she would be using – as they slid it underneath Fortis. It was big enough to support him, just, then they had to pick up the corners, one on each side and lift him up. He was too weak to help himself and Minna thought he might well die before they got him home. If she didn't pass out first... It was terrible finding a footing over the marsh without stumbling. She had already used her day's strength! But Cerdic was strong and picked out the best way and soon they were struggling off the marsh and onto the flat grazed grass. The fort did not look too far away.

"I can go and get help, if you want," Cerdic said as they rested. "If it's too much for you."

"No. I can manage." She spoke despairingly, knowing she must summon the last reserves of her strength. The hound was so heavy! But he was dying. "We must get him to the warmth as soon as possible. We mustn't waste time."

She was hopeful, as Fortis lifted his head and waved his tail again. They had given him heart, she thought, and the will to live, but he was desperately weak. He still might die.

Tiberius, fortunately, was an abstemious man and had no wish to stay up all night. He retired to the guest's quarters before midnight, and Theo ordered the slaves to find comfortable berths for his retinue. When they had all departed and silence descended on the now cool, high-roofed atrium, Theo stayed in his place at the table with only Benoc waiting silently behind him. One lamp alone still burned, its golden light contrasting with the cold bright moonlight that shone in from the courtyard.

"Why did Cerdic and Minna leave?"

His voice echoed through the empty hall.

"They have gone to search for the hound's body," Benoc said.

Theo nodded. "Of course…poor Cerdic. As well the horse did not drown…" he murmured, and smiled. And sighed.

Then he stood up. "Fetch me my clothes. Unwind me from my finery. I can scarce walk."

Benoc knew the difficult ways of the toga and expertly stripped Theo from the swathes of fine white wool and brought him his old tunic and leather jerkin and outdoor cloak.

"Wait up," Theo commanded.

Benoc bowed.

Theo went out to the porch of the atrium and stood for a moment on the steps, looking at the stars. Was his fate written up there, as many believed? Which of the various paths his life might take? He knew he had to do as he was ordered, not much different from Benoc, but to wine and dine Tiberius to the best of his ability was to make a friend of the man who had the power over him. He had gone out of his way; the day had gone well and his success would stand him in good stead. Praise to the gods, that Tiberius was going to sleep full of goodwill towards his subordinate!

But so much had depended on Minna, that little slip of thunder and lightning with her beetle brows of fury and the smile of a spring sun bursting out of a cloud: he never could work out what his feelings were towards her! He tried not to give the subject too much thought; it was dangerous. But he owed it to her now, after what she had achieved…she needed his kindness. He was only too well aware of what he meant to her. But she to him? He shook his head, as ever pushing the thought away. Best to leave it as it had always been: childhood friends, close and loyal, but no more.

He went out by the west gate. The guard, bad-tempered to be on duty this night of celebration, jumped, startled, to salute him. Theo threw him a goodnight and turned along the west wall to make for the marshes. The men were still carousing in the vicus but the way ahead of him was empty, scoured to the horizon by the eternal coming and going of the tide. The passage of the sea was a law unto itself, never to be tamed, however clever man might be. If it gave up the body of a drowned dog it would be a miracle.

He walked on southward, only guessing as to which way the searchers might have gone. It was not so important: the fine night air and the full moon gave him the solace his overwrought brain needed. He was seldom alone. The feel of the springy grass as he skirted the high-tide mark, the fresh smell of the sea and the mud after the odours of the packed fort, were balm to his spirit. He was filled with a fine optimism for what might lie ahead, aware suddenly of how privileged he was. The lad Benoc might as well have been an ox for all the say he had over his life, while he, Theodosius Valerian Aquila, had been steered by the gods to the fringe of greatness, with fantastic opportunities at his fingertips if he played his cards right. And yet they had been born in similar circumstances. Truly, the gods had favoured him! (He must be nicer to Benoc, he thought, while he was overwhelmed by these fine thoughts. He forgot later.)

But then in the moonlight ahead he saw something move. He stopped, his hand going instinctively to the sword which swung at his side. His first thought was that it was one of the marauders – a few had escaped the round-up, he was pretty sure – but then his sharp eyes made out two figures, apparently staggering. It could only be Cerdic and Minna. Incredible if they had found the hound! He altered course, suddenly eager for their company.

"Minna! Cerdic!"

To Minna it was as if Jupiter himself had come down from the sky – to look up at the shout and see Theo's familiar figure swinging towards them in the moonlight! In his light step she recognized the strength they so badly needed. Her own had all run out; she was near fainting.

"Oh, Theo – help us! He is so heavy. We – I – can't – I can't –" Her voice broke with a sob.

"He's still alive?" Theo dropped to his knees, putting his hand out for Fortis to sniff. "Amazing! The gods are with him, I think. Here, let me –"

Carefully he got his hands under the hound's body, gathered him into his arms and, with an effort, straightened up onto his feet.

"By Jupiter, he's a weight!"

"Can you carry him?"

"Yes, as far as the fort, I think."

"He knows you've come to save him," Cerdic said. "Look at his tail waving! He has the will to live now – he will be all right!"

Cerdic was so excited at their good fortune that he was talking to Theo as if they were boys out to play, like old times. Minna stumbled to her feet, feeling her tears turning into laughter. If only she were Fortis, safe in Theo's arms! How wonderful that would be! But the sight of his graceful figure ahead of her, dark against the starry sky, revived her from total exhaustion. She stumbled up beside him.

"How lucky you came! We didn't think we could carry him between us."

"I only came out for peace and fresh air!"

"I couldn't have done any more, my strength is all gone. "

"You used it to good effect, Minna. I'm proud of

you. It's a pity we can't have girls in the army. You would be a centurion in no time."

She laughed. Her mind whirled with confusion, delight, despair. The day seemed to have lasted for ever.

Theo carried the hound all the way back to the blacksmith's shop in the fort. Minna's mother was still gossiping with her friends, waiting up for Minna, and her father had just come back from his gaming. They all jumped up in shock at the sudden entry of the commander.

"Look, we have Fortis, and he's alive! He's still alive!" Cerdic called out.

Theo kneeled down and laid the hound on the cushions the women had been sitting on and rested a moment, still kneeling. As the women exclaimed and scurried to fetch him honeyed wine, and to fire up the brazier to warm milk for the dog, he felt suddenly that he was back in his childhood with his old playmates, in the warmth of a real house – no ceremony, no fawning slaves, no cold seclusion. He was momentarily back in a family, a state he had almost forgotten. It brought him a rush of emotion, remembering his parents, hugs and kisses and quarrels, even beatings – how it had been once. The memory flooded his weary brain and as quickly receded, leaving him strangely shaken. His own villa awaiting him was empty and cold. He longed to lie down beside Fortis and go to sleep in this rackety little house behind the forge, Minna's home.

He decided he had drunk too much wine.

"Goodnight to you," he said. "I trust the hound will thrive."

He turned and was gone.

Minna took a step after him, hesitated, caught her mother's eye, and sank down on the couch. Her head was whirling.

"Go to bed now. Cerdic has to go back to barracks. I will tend the hound, don't worry. You did well to find him."

Minna lay down. The women left and Cerdic and his mother cleaned and fed Fortis. The blacksmith was already snoring. Minna heard her mother say her prayers to Ceres and climb into bed beside her father, and then all was silent. Cerdic lay on his stomach beside Fortis, whispering to him, watching the spark come back into the golden-brown eyes. He licked Cerdic's fingers and made some whimpers of love. Minna could not sleep.

"How lucky we've been today, Cerdic! Both of us, you and me. How it turned out well for you after all, coming back. And for me, going on. And now, finding Fortis alive! I think the gods are smiling on us."

"I'm on duty at dawn – I won't feel they are smiling then! But yes, finding Fortis alive – I never dreamed that was possible."

They were closer now, brother and sister, than they had been since they were children. They were both aware of it, but did not put the feelings into words. Minna stood up, stretched. She was beyond sleep now.

She went out and walked up the road through the fort. It was quiet now, everyone asleep save for the guard and the watch-outs on the ramparts. Even the prisoners who faced death were silent in the fort jail. Minna knew she was treading in Theo's footsteps, drawn as by a magnet. But when she got to his villa she passed on, because there was no place for her there. The guards on the doorway watched impassively.

She slipped into the doorway of the now silent barracks and down a passage to the stables. The soldiers slept with their horses, and she knew now that she would too. Silva was lying down and gave a soft whicker as she came to him. He stretched out his muzzle to her. Like Fortis, he offered his love with a soft nosing at her hand. Minna lay down in the straw and laid her head on the warm flank.

And slept.

MINNA'S JOURNEY

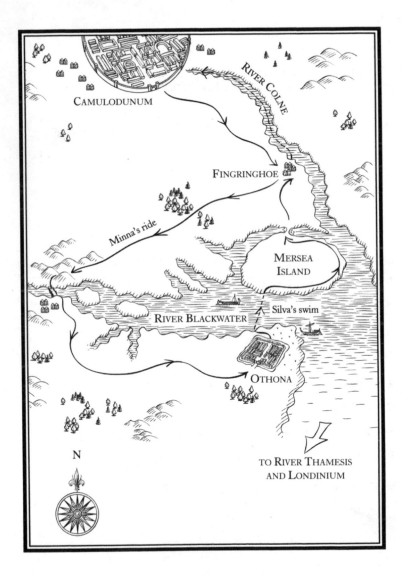

GLOSSARY

amphitheatre – a round, open, public building with tiers of seats surrounding a central space for spectator sports, games and displays

amphora – a tall jar or jug with two handles and a narrow neck

atrium – the main area of a Roman house with rooms opening off it

Belgica – in Roman times, an area of northern Europe, including what is now Belgium

Camulodunum – Colchester, Essex

Caesaromagus – Chelmsford, Essex

centurion – a professional officer of the Roman army, who usually commanded about eighty men

Ceres – the Roman goddess of the grain and the harvest

Claudius – Roman Emperor from AD41–54

Constantine I – Roman Emperor from AD306–337

cuddy – a small cabin on a ship or boat

Fingringhoe – a small river port which served the Roman colony at Camulodunum

Germania – in Roman times, an area of northern Europe, including what is now Germany

Hadrian – Roman emperor from AD117–138, who ordered the construction of a great wall to safeguard northern England against invasion from Caledonia (Scotland)

hypocaust – Roman system of central heating. The floor was raised off the ground by pillars, and spaces were left inside the walls so that hot air from a furnace could circulate

Jupiter – the chief god in Roman mythology, in charge of laws and social order. The Roman counterpart of Zeus, the sky father who sends thunder and lightning

Londinium – London

Magnentius – Roman commander who attempted to usurp the Roman Empire in AD350–353

Mithras – the god of Mithraism, an Eastern Mediterranean religion practised in the Roman Empire, particularly popular with soldiers

Othona – a Roman fort which was located in an isolated area of what is now Essex

Silvanus – the Roman god of wild nature, uncultivated land, forests and hunting

Thamesis – the River Thames

tribune – a high-ranking official in either the army or government

triclinium – a room used to entertain company, where diners would recline and eat around three sides of a low square table

vicus (plural vici) – a civilian settlement which grew up close to a Roman military garrison

Zeus – the chief god in Greek mythology, god of the sky and thunder

Usborne Quicklinks

For links to websites where you can find out more about Roman life in Britain, learn how to make authentic honey cakes, and see pictures of what Colchester (Camulodunum) would have looked like in Roman times, go to the Usborne Quicklinks Website at www.usborne-quicklinks.com and enter the keywords "minna's quest".

Internet safety
When using the Internet, make sure you follow these safety guidelines:
- Ask an adult's permission before using the Internet.
- Never give out personal information, such as your name, address or telephone number.
- If a website asks you to type in your name or e-mail address, check with an adult first.
- If you receive an e-mail from someone you don't know, don't reply to it.

Usborne Publishing is not responsible and does not accept liability for the availability or content of any website other than its own, or for any exposure to harmful, offensive, or inaccurate material which may appear on the Web. Usborne Publishing will have no liability for any damage or loss caused by viruses that may be downloaded as a result of browsing the sites it recommends. We recommend that children are supervised while on the Internet.